LOST SECRET

THE KISS CHRONICLES, BOOK 1

EMILY REED

PROLOGUE

My DYING sister vanished in the middle of the night. Usually, Megan called to me before dawn, but sunshine pooled on the bare wood floor beneath the window when I woke.

My heart leapt into my throat. *She's dead. After months of fighting, Megan finally...*I hadn't felt it though. Wouldn't I *know* if the only person I ever loved—

I stumbled out of bed, tangling in my blankets, then raced to her room. *Empty.* The sheets were folded aside. She must be close. I moved down the hall toward our shared bathroom. The door stood open, but Megan wasn't there.

Backtracking, I checked the living room with its slouchy couches, and the kitchen with its worn countertops. *No Megan.* I pushed through the French doors out onto our balcony.

The music district of Crescent City, a night owl's paradise, lay still in the soft morning light. Megan's flowers overflowed their boxes, spilling riotous colors down the wrought iron rail. I stood alone, a gentle breeze lifted a lock of my hair, and tears stung my eyes. *Megan was gone.*

The police assumed she left of her own free will—there was no evidence of a break-in or struggle. "Maybe she was done fighting and couldn't tell you," the detective said, his brown eyes sympathetic.

"You didn't know her, she would *never* give up."

"Often when people go missing, the loved ones they leave behind come to realize," he paused and took a breath, "that they didn't know them as well as they thought. *Everyone has secrets, Darling,*" his voice drawled over my name.

"Megan could barely walk," I ground out. "Somebody must have *taken* her."

"But who would kidnap a dying young woman? How did they leave no evidence? Why didn't you hear them?" He asked. I didn't have any answers.

It didn't make sense. Nothing did anymore.

Strange, exhilarating dreams began haunting my nights. A new hunger, an unquenchable thirst that felt almost...*dangerous*...ruled my days.

Scared and alone, I couldn't imagine the dark secrets my hunger hid. They'd been lost for so long—locked away, buried by time, and twisted by whispered lies—but when Megan was stolen everything began to unravel...

Before it did, before I saw the dead rise, witnessed vampires feed, or visited the warlocks' library, *before I held a life at the edge of my lips*, I was just Darling Price—a musician like so many others in this vibrant city. I struggled to pay bills, practiced with my band, and grieved for my missing sister. I was innocent and naive.

I'd barely even been kissed.

CHAPTER ONE

Leaves trailed wet along my spine, soaking through the thin night shirt as I ducked under a tree bow. A shiver from the icy sensation broke goosebumps across my skin. Sticks and pebbles dug at my bare feet with every step.

Fear urged me forward. But I needed to be quiet, *have to hide, can't let them discover me.*

Moonlight beamed through a break in the cloud cover, reflecting off dew dropped foliage. My breath bloomed white in front of me.

Glancing over my shoulder I saw nothing but the shifting forest, the trees and underbrush blending together like a black on black charcoal drawing—the blue hue of the moon providing the only sense of edges. Wet soil and decayed leaves scented the air. *Without death there is no life. Energy never ends, it just changes shape.*

Turning forward again, I stopped short. A fire flickered between the trees. A step back, another, and I hit a tree, knocking my teeth together.

Terror stabbed at me, a physical force, painful in its ferocity. A whimper escaped—fear given voice.

I interlaced my fingers, squeezing the knuckles together until they hurt, draining the pain from my fear into something I controlled.

I need something. Something is missing. Without it I'll remain broken forever.

A snowflake drifted in front of me, slow yet purposeful: gravity forced its destination but did not control its journey. The flake disappeared into the darkness at my feet.

A sound drew my attention back to the fire. Movement between the trees—a figure circled the flames. My heartbeat thumped in my throat. I clenched my jaw so hard it ached.

The snow thickened, stinging cold on my face. I wet my lips, tasting the frozen rain—icy and familiar. *Home.*

The person beyond the trees stopped walking, standing still, the fire silhouetting them. I squinted but couldn't make out the figure clearly. Didn't know if it was a man or woman. Didn't know why they terrified me.

The figure turned suddenly, glittering eyes—the moonlight caught in frozen dew—pinning me in place. "You enter my realm, child?" it asked, the gravelly voice sounding close, right next to my ear—the warmth of breath on my neck startled me into action.

Turning, I ran, sprinting through the forest, my hands grabbing at trees, pulling myself forward and pushing off them, finding a path through the twisting landscape—some branches helped me forward, others dragged at me. *A war brews between powerful forces and I am locked in the middle.*

The night shifted to day, and my running transformed into stillness.

I stood in a stream, the freezing water rushing over my feet, splashing around my calves.

Smooth colorful stones, made bright and shiny by the water and sunshine, lined the stream bed. Trees bursting with fall foliage bordered the bank, leaning toward the ice cold water that numbed my feet.

A chill raced over my skin but it wasn't from the water. I scanned the forest, searching through the thick foliage for movement. *Something is watching me.* A hot gust of wind picked up my hair, pushing it over my shoulders and streaming it along the sides of my face. I turned and my breath caught in my throat.

A man stood at the water's edge, shirtless. He stared at me with eyes of blue green that shone with an unnatural light—no one should have eyes that sparkly.

His lips tilted into a half smile, revealing a dimple. High sculpted cheekbones, and pitch black hair framed the eyes. *He is familiar.*

My gaze ran over his broad shoulders and across his collar bones. The salty taste of his skin bloomed in my mouth. *How?*

The tattoo on his abdomen, a black wheel with spokes inscribed in a script I couldn't read, shifted with his movement as he took a step into the water.

His hands flexed at his side, the fingers brushing his indigo jeans.

"Hi," he said, his smile broadening. He tilted his head in question.

"Who are you?" I asked.

"You called me with your song."

"Which one?"

Chords of music drifted to me. A song I'd written with my best friend, Megan… before she disappeared.

"What's your name?" I asked.

He shook his head just a little. "That I can't tell you."

The ground trembled, the stones under my feet shifting. I put my hands out for balance. My nightshirt slipped off one shoulder. When I looked back at the beautiful, familiar stranger, he was focused on the newly exposed bare skin.

I pulled the shirt up, covering myself, holding the soft fabric close to my neck. His gaze flicked to mine. "There is no need for shyness between us," he said. *Says you.*

He smiled and the world shifted again, growing hazy and soft.

His hand slipped over my skin, soft but not careful. He was never careful…but always tender.

We'd known each other since the beginning of time. And we would be together until the end.

His lips met mine, nourishing me.

I needed him—loved him. Would never be whole without him.

My body arched, desperate to be closer, to be one.

He smiled against my lips, teasing me with his touch. He whispered my name and I opened my mouth to say his…

I woke twisted in my sheets. *Another dream.* Reaching out towards my bedside table, I grabbed my dream diary, knocking my pen to the floor in the process. *Crud.* My long dark hair draped to the floor when I grabbed it. By the time I touched the pen to paper, the details of the dream had faded to just feelings: emptiness and dread with a side helping of sexual frustration. *Awesomesauce.*

This happened almost every night since Megan disappeared two months ago.

I climbed out of bed, the dream drifting away as it always did. On my way to the bathroom I stopped at Megan's bedroom and leaned against the doorjamb.

Her dark wood dressing table was covered in medication. I'd lined up the pill bottles, and there they sat, like little soldiers, waiting for their mistress to return. Polaroid pictures, squares of color with Megan's red hair the unifying theme, were tucked into the frame of the mirror.

I can still smell her perfume. Crossing the room to her chest of drawers, I picked up the small bottle of Gilt. The smell wafted up, and I closed my eyes, sensing her there.

She'd worn it since we moved to Crescent City. Before we had a place to live, before we got our first gig, Megan bought a bottle. She paid for it with the money we earned playing on the streets. And I never questioned her. She was a star. Megan knew her path; my only job was to follow.

Flyers from our performances and clippings about our band hung on the wall. Even in the grainy black and white ones, Megan glowed. Leaning over the microphone, her hair falling long to one side, exposing her profile, mouth wide, neck extended, eyes squeezed shut—you could almost hear how powerful her voice was through the paper. Megan sang until there was nothing left.

I was in the photos too, but always in the background, my hair flopped over my face, fingers tense on the strings of my fiddle. Megan was the star, and I a moon lucky enough to orbit her.

Replacing the bottle of perfume on the dresser next to a pair of dangly earrings, I sat on the bed, smoothing the quilt. Megan left the bed unmade, and I didn't fix it until days after she disappeared. I couldn't stand walking by the door and seeing it like that, as if she would be back any minute. *She vanished in the middle of the night. How does a dying woman disappear?*

I fished under the bed and pulled out Megan's other box of clippings. The ones on top, yellow and curled with age, were cut out of the local paper up north. They told the story of the early and tragic death of a much beloved choir instructor, Mr. Man.

He'd led the school to great glory that year, winning the regional championships. Megan Quick, 13, his foster daughter, was the star of the show. In his obituary photo, Mr. Man's thick hair was parted to the side; he wore a crisp white shirt and a dark narrow tie. There was a glint in his eye and a tilt to his chin that implied devilish fun.

When he died, only white fluff clung to the sides of his head. His illness drained him, sucking the skin around his eyes into the hollows. Those once-bright orbs of light became dull and confused in the final months. It took almost a year for Mr. Man to die. At the end, people whispered that his passing was a blessing.

Later articles, printed off microfiche from the Crescent City library, followed up with the disappearance of two of his foster children. Thirteen-year-old girls, much missed and worried about by his widow. One, Darling Price, suffered from a delusional disorder, the paper informed its readers. Without her medication, she could slip into a psychotic state. *They got that wrong.* I left those pills behind and hadn't hallucinated since.

I looked at the date on the article. We left two days before it made the paper. Megan and I were riding trains, headed south to the only place Megan thought would be right for us, Crescent City.

We trundled through a dark and dismal landscape lined with chain-link fence. I started to cry. Megan came over to where I sat, huddled against some burlap sacks filled with grain.

"Darling, you don't have to be afraid." I nodded, but the tears continue. "You're safe now. He can't hurt us anymore."

"But, Megan," I hiccupped. "Won't I go to hell?"

Megan's brow furrowed deeply and her eyes flashed in the dark. "Of course not."

"But it's my fault, Megan."

"No, it isn't. He deserved to die, so he got sick and died. That's what happens to bad people. That's proof that God is watching."

"No, Megan." I took a shuddering breath. "You don't understand, I wanted him to die."

"So. Did. I."

"It was when his chest hair turned gray. I knew that if I didn't stop, he would die. I was offered a sign, a chance, but I kept going."

Megan frowned. "You didn't do anything, Darling. He was the one doing it. And even if you did kill him—you still wouldn't be going to hell. You saved us both, Darling." My sobs became uncontrollable.

Megan pulled a knife out of her bag. It flashed for a second before she sliced it across her palm. She grabbed mine and did the same. The sharp sensation snapped me out of my tears, and I stared at the blood, not feeling any pain. Megan pressed her bleeding palm to mine.

"Listen to me, Darling." I nodded. *"You will be okay. We will stay together forever. This is a blood pact. If you go to hell, I will be there with you. I'll never leave you alone. You are safe with me, and I am safe with you."* I nodded. *"Say it."*

"I am safe with you—"

"And you are safe with me."

"And you are safe with me."

"Forever."

"Forever."

I could almost hear her voice as I sat on the bed looking down at the clippings. I recognized the powerful young woman who'd promised me safety. She was all over the walls of this room; she lived in the hearts and minds of fans all over the city. *But she left me.* She didn't even say goodbye.

Tears hit the papers on my lap. I curled up into a ball and sobbed into her pillow, letting the grief rack through me. *How many times have I done this, just curled up on her bed and lost it?*

The grief came in waves. One minute I'd feel almost normal, and the next I'd be crushed by it. *Utterly destroyed.* Absence is a heavy thing. How can something that isn't there weigh so damn much!

My phone beeped in the other room. I ignored it, not ready to pull out of my misery. My phone chimed again. I took a deep breath and opened my swollen eyes to check the time. *I'm due at the hospital in an hour then I have band practice right after. Time to get my butt out of bed.*

Sniffling and wiping at my face, I returned the papers to their box, letting my finger run over Megan's face before replacing the lid and slipping it under the bed. I straightened Megan's quilt and stared down at the pattern, letting the colors and shapes blur in my vision. The pain and sorrow dragged at me, draining me of every last drop. *I am dangerously empty.*

CHAPTER TWO

When I entered the hospital lobby, the smell of it dropped me back into every walk Megan and I took through this place, into every battle we waged. *We never won.*

I rode the elevator with a wheelchair-bound man and young woman. They shared the same thin noses and full lips. Both looked drawn, their cheeks sunken and hair limp. *She's his primary care giver. I can always recognize them.* They look like crap—slumped shoulders and heavy bags hanging under their eyes. Skin only a little brighter than their loved ones deathly pallor.

Not me, though. As Megan grew gaunt, I filled out, my hips and ass growing plumper, my waist narrowing, breasts rising so that now I hardly owned a shirt that contained them. My lips were pink, cheeks flushed, eyes bright. As Megan died, I grew stronger and healthier. *It didn't make sense.*

The doors opened and air, heavy with disinfectant, wafted in.

Tingling along my spine turned my head as I stepped off. Piercing bright blue eyes waited for me. The intensity of the stranger's gaze tightened my throat. The elevator doors closed behind me and suddenly it was just me and this man alone in the hall.

He wore an elegant grey three piece suit with thin threads of blue running through it. The vest stretched across a hard chest, and tapered to a narrowed waist. No tie, just an open collar that exposed the notch between his collar bones.

A deliciously slow smile curled his lips, and a cruel spark came into his gaze. *No man's lips should be so pink, or skin so alabaster. No stranger should look at me with such unabashed hunger. How can he be so pretty and so masculine?*

He stalked toward me, the suit moving with him like a second skin. I stumbled back, adrenaline pumping into my system. My body thrummed with a bizarre anticipation—I wanted him to grab me. To do something. *I want. Want. But what?*

His long stride ate up the space between us but he stopped five feet shy, his gaze never leaving my face. The smile faded from that too pretty mouth—how could lips the color of dusty rose send shivers of warning down my spine?

We stared at each other for a long moment, time seeming to stretch. The bustle of the hospital went silent. My heartbeat louder than any noise. He shook his head slightly, as if coming to some private conclusion then pushed into the stairwell door and disappeared.

I stood alone in the hall, heart hammering, breath uneven, cheeks hot —all kinds of confused and freaked out.

What the what was that?

The door next to me opened and a patient came out, breaking me from my trance.

Claire and Harriet sat behind the check in desk. A similar height and weight, it took several visits for me to tell the two nurses apart—Harriet had a small scar on her lip.

They stared at the news playing on a TV mounted in the corner of the waiting room. "The victims of the attack were brought to Mercy Hospital at approximately 4 a.m. The first victim had seizures soon after admittance," the announcer announced.

The video switched to a bird's-eye view of a city street. Yellow tarps covered two bodies and dark smears stained the cement. "Witnesses say that this woman"—the screen switched to a mug shot: a white woman, spiked bleached blonde hair, chin raised so she looked down her nose at the camera—"Angela Hoppenheimer, who has prior arrests for prostitution and drug possession, attacked the men as they walked home from an evening out with friends."

It cut back to the anchor. He held a finger to his ear for a moment.

"Now we are going live to a press conference with the chief of Crescent City Security."

The screen switched to a stout woman in her fifties standing at a podium. "As you all know, there was another attack yesterday in the early evening. While this incident is still under investigation, we ask for your patience and perseverance. We believe that a newer form of hallucinogen on the market is causing these attacks," she said. "Citizens of Crescent City, if you encounter a person on this drug, acting erratically, violent"— she cleared her throat—"insatiably hungry, call the police. Do not attempt to engage them."

A reporter yelled a question. The chief answered it. "We are not sure why the victims of these attacks are having seizures and exhibiting other side effects. That is something we are working closely with the doctors over at Mercy to figure out."

Another unintelligible question.

"It is believed to be a drug, not a virus, causing these attacks, so we have not reached out to the CCA."

"Do you plan on canceling the annual zombie run?" a reporter in the front row asked, his mouth close enough to the mic for the audience to hear.

"No," she smiled. "These are not zombies."

"They brought the victims here?" I asked.

The nurses turned, noticing my presence for the first time. "Oh, hi, Darling," Claire said. "Yes," she answered, her voice turning grave. "They came in late last night."

"Terrible," I mumbled, casting my eyes to the floor.

"How are you?" Harriet pitched her voice upward, her tone implying that it was almost impossible for me to be doing well. And if I was in good shape, it was a struggle. She expected a sad smile, a brave face.

I looked up at her, making eye contact.

She startled, her eyes slowly growing glassy as I held her gaze. "I'm fine." I shifted my focus back to the floor, looking at my sneakers. "I've got an appointment."

"Yes," Claire said. "I saw that. So brave of you."

I kept my eyes on the ground as I shrugged. "If I can help." This was my fourth bone marrow harvest. When the doctors suggested the treatment for Megan, they tested me, but I wasn't a match for her. However, I matched a lot of other people. In fact, I was a record-breaker. I'd had a surgery every three months since then.

Harriet clicked her tongue against her teeth. "Let's get you checked in," she said. "Oh, you're seeing Dr. Tor," she looked over at Claire. They smiled at each other, their eyes alight with humor. Harriet returned her gaze to her screen. "He's new," she told me, "and I think he's from the Federation of Kingdoms."

"I thought further east," Claire said. "Either way." She smiled at me. "He's a nice young doctor." Then she nodded. *Got it—I should date the nice new doctor.* I gave her a tight-lipped smile. Too bad I don't date.

His hair was so black that light seemed to be absorbed by it. *He must run his fingers through it a lot. That's probably why it's slightly disheveled and pushed off his forehead in that mad scientist look.* But he was young, his skin the color of wheat fields glowing golden in the light of a setting sun, and unlined. Mad scientist have wrinkles…from all the stress of insanity.

"I'm Dr. Issa Tor," he smiled, his accent slight and yet distinctly foreign. He waved a long arm toward the examination table. "Have a seat."

The paper crinkled when I climbed on it. Dr. Tor sat on a low-wheeled stool entering passwords and reading warning boxes that sprang up his screen.

"Thank you for donating again. Your marrow is very rare." His eyes stayed focused on the screen. "I don't see a family history here." He turned to me, his eyebrows raised. "You were adopted?"

"Something like that."

He cocked his head, and I thought he might ask me more questions, but he just turned back to the screen.

"What is the disease this time?" I asked looking down at my sneakers.

"Leukemia, so a harvest," he answered, turning back to me. "Are you up for it?"

"Yes," I said. "I'll be fine."

He pushed off with one of his long legs and rolled the stool to where a blood pressure cuff hung. Dr. Tor held his stethoscope up to his mouth and breathes on it. When the metal touched my skin it was warm; his fingers did not brush me, but I wanted them to.

A war brews inside me, battling between an intense need to be left alone and a hunger for touch.

Dr. Tor pulled out his earbuds and returned the stethoscope to his neck. "Good." The many textured sound of the Velcro from the blood pressure cuff ripping loose rasped against my skin sending a delicious shudder through me.

The doctor returned to his computer. Each stroke on the keyboard made a satisfying clack.

"I'm hoping we can do this early next week; we've got all your paperwork, everything is matching up." He nodded at the computer. "Same address?" he asked.

"Yes."

"Phone number?"

"Yup."

"Emergency contact here is Megan Quick. Is her number still the same?"

I gripped the edge of the table, my hands pressing hard into the padding. "She's gone," I said.

"Moved?" he asked, not taking his eyes off the screen. "We've got her as the same address as you, but I can change that." He clacked some more.

"Disappeared," I squeezed the word from between my lips, trying to keep the truth out of the air I breathed.

He looked over from the computer, his eyebrows raised in question.

"She was a patient here," I said.

His expression shifted from confused to embarrassed, his cheeks flushing and eyes lowering. "I'm sorry," he said. "For your loss."

"I'll just get a cab home after."

He looked up at me, his skin still flushed but eyes intent. "We don't recommend that."

"I know the recommendations," I said through gritted teeth. "I know all about your recommendations." I bit down on my lip to stop the anger bubbling out of me. *Megan and I followed them all, and she still wasted away.*

Closing my eyes, I took a deep breath then blew it out through slightly parted lips, letting my jaw relax. "I'm sorry," I said. "Can we just finish up here? I've got to go."

"Of course," he turned back to his computer. "You're not on any medications?" I shook my head. "You used to be on antipsychotics, though?"

"Not for a long time. Is that in the records there?" I had not taken any medication regularly since moving to Crescent City. *Why would Mercy have my records from before I moved here?*

"Our system was recently upgraded," Dr. Tor said. "It links to any other facility records with a matching name and ID number."

"Oh," I said. "I haven't taken anything like that in a long time. Would it matter if I did?"

Dr. Tor shrugged. "It's not a problem either way."

"I had a messed-up childhood," I blurted out. Dr. Tor nodded and raised his eyebrows, encouraging me to continue. "They said I had false memories." *I can't believe I'm telling him this.* But the words spilled out of me as if drawn by some kind of spell. "I have not hallucinated in a long time."

"What did you hallucinate?" He asked, leaning slightly forward on his stool, the metal creaking beneath him.

"I–" A knock on the door interrupted me and Harriet walked in, holding a file. A blush ran up my chest and over my throat. *I almost told him about my delusions!*

Harriet passed the file to Dr. Tor. I glanced at my phone; it was later than I thought.

"I have to go," I said.

Harriet closed the door behind her even as I reached for it. Dr. Tor stood quickly. "Please, Darling, I just need a few more minutes."

"I'm sorry, but I'll be late for band practice. I have to go."

"But you'll come back? For the surgery, I mean." He ran a hand through that dark hair, his eyes—just a few shades darker than his skin... wheat under a stromy sky—focused on my chin. As if he didn't want to meet my gaze.

"Of course." He raised his eyes then and I wasn't ready. His breath stopped, and his pupils dilated. I turned and yanked open the door. *My emptiness can suck in others. I am dangerous.*

CHAPTER THREE

I HURRIED TO BAND PRACTICE. *If you don't have talent, at least you can cultivate punctuality.* Michael, our lead singer, nodded when I walked in and checked his watch. *Didn't bother with a smile.*

We'd been working together since Megan got really sick—a few months before she disappeared. I didn't want to play with anyone else, but we had bills to pay. It wasn't hard to find someone who would take me. Like a good moon, I reflected the light of my sun beautifully.

The practice space belonged to our bassist, Emmanuel, who never showed up on time. He saw Megan and me play a couple of times and invited me to join Higgs and The Bosons. I had a feeling he regretted it. Judging by Michael's sour expression, he definitely did. *Without Megan I suck.*

Our drummer, Andrew, nodded to me as he walked in. A tall, lanky guy who looked good in a worn T-shirt, he had floppy hair that danced around his head when he played.

I tuned my violin, listening to the instrument, asking it to speak to me. We used to make magic—Megan, my fiddle, and me. Now I just practiced. Nothing special ever came through me.

My throat tightened and pressure built behind my eyes. I put the instrument down and leaned against the wall, taking deep even breaths. *Pull it together.*

Megan always stressed how we had to believe in ourselves. In our talent. *"We have to have faith, Darling. We can do this!"*

We.

A searing anger burned away the unshed tears. *How could she leave me!*

"You okay?" Emmanuel leaned against the wall next to me, his stance casual. I swallowed and pressed my lips together, taking in another breath through my nose before looking up at him.

His black curls, untrimmed and wild, floated around his head like a crown. His mahogany eyes flashed with amethyst. I dropped my gaze to his perfectly formed lips. *They look so soft surrounded by that dark, rough stubble.* "Are you sure?" he asked.

Something about the question made the damn tears come back. *Crap.* I turned away, trying to hide from him.

"Everyone's here, so let's get started," Michael announced.

"Just a minute." Emmanuel stepped closer, his breath warm on my shoulder. "You will be okay, Darling." My name in his voice settled me—like a solid, comforting hand on my back. I peeked at him through my hair, keeping a black veil between us. He smiled gently, more with his eyes than mouth.

"You ready to play?" Michael asked, an edge in his voice.

Emmanuel nodded, and I felt my head moving with his. He stepped back, those smiling eyes holding mine for a beat before he picked up his bass and hung the strap across his broad shoulders.

My gaze fell to his forearms, the muscles sharpening as he held the instrument. I licked my lips, hunger churning in my gut at the sight of Emmanuel's long elegant fingers pressing and strumming the strings.

"Darling?" Michael said. "Uh, can we have the pleasure of your company today?"

"Sure," I said, barely above a whisper.

"Let's start with 'Drawn to You'," Michael suggested.

Andrew counted off a "one, two, three," clacking his sticks together. Emmanuel laid down the bass while Dre thumped out the beat. I pulled my bow against the strings, eyes closed, trying to invoke the music that belonged there. The notes came, but without the feeling, it sounded drab and flat.

That's how practice went. All the boys played with their hearts, and I struggled not to miss anything. We practiced our whole set several times, paying particular attention to the single we planned to open with at our next gig. Our manager promised a couple of important people were coming to see us. The scent of a record contract floated in the air.

As the last song ended, Michael glared at me, his eyes slits of anger. "What the fuck?" he asked.

"Hey!" Emmanuel tensed.

Michael turned on him. "She's fucking it up, Emmanuel."

Emmanuel, his bass still hanging from his shoulders, stepped in front of Michael, blocking my view of him. "Lay off her." His voice was a quiet threat.

"It was your idea to invite her; you fix her." Anger wafted off him. I kept my eyes down, concentrating on the grain of my indigo jeans. He snorted before stomping to the door. It slammed shut behind him.

I returned my fiddle to the case and closed the clasps—so upset I couldn't even enjoy the clicking sound they made. As I stood, Emmanuel approached me, his hands in the pockets of his jeans, his bass left in its stand. "You ever been to the Villa Relma Cemetery?" he asked.

Huh? "I've passed it. Why?"

Villa Relma was one of the city's more popular cemeteries. Tourists flocked there to see the graves of some of the area's most notorious residents. It wasn't big, but within the crumbling walls laid three mayors, a famous priestess, and one of the biggest movie stars of the last century.

"You want to go? With me? Now?" he asked, his eyes cast down, hiding under his dark lashes...letting me admire his high cheekbones and strong jaw, the contrast of his soft lips against that rough stubble again. I suppressed a sigh. "It's a place I've always found comforting."

I didn't have time to look away before his eyes locked onto mine. I was drawn toward him, sinking into his gaze. "So what do you say? Want to go?"

"Okay," I took a tentative step toward him. He broke eye contact and, reaching down, grabbed my violin case before turning to the exit. I followed him, tripping over myself a little. *I should really eat something.*

CHAPTER FOUR

WE ENTERED Villa Relma Cemetery as darkness fell. A cooling breeze accompanied the setting sun. Summer filled the air with heat and moisture during the day but the night still belonged to the spring.

Emmanuel knew his way around, and I followed between the rows of mausoleums and crypts. Some were crumbling to the ground. The metal fences around them collapsed under fallen chunks of the structures they were meant to protect. Spurts of growth, green and ragged, shot from between the bricks, reaching toward the sun, making life work where it could.

Tourist and locals wandered among the graves.

Emmanuel led me to an unfenced, squat mausoleum about my height. Black dirt clung to the texture of the cement facade and gathered in the cracks. The entire thing was covered in question marks. They were written in groups of three question marks, some small and tight, others scrawled.

Candles, beaded necklaces, and mini bottles of liquor covered the roof's edge and lined the base. Envelopes and folded scraps of paper leaned against the worn, unreadable, marble plaque where it met the cemetery path.

Emmanuel's shoulders shifted underneath his thin T-shirt as he placed my violin case on the ground. He reached into the pocket of his worn jeans and pulled out a couple of pennies and two sugar packets, holding them out in his palm toward me.

His dark curls fell around his face as he looked down at me. *We are in a fort together, no one can see us.* Emmanuel smiled shyly. "Go ahead," he said. "Take a penny and a sugar packet and offer it to her."

"Who?"

"Suki, a powerful spirit. I think she can help you."

I looked over at the shrine. "You really believe in this kind of stuff?" I asked.

He shrugged. "Can't hurt. I guess it's—I don't know." I glanced at him. He looked at the mausoleum, the sun behind him backlighting his profile and turning his hair into a halo. "She's helped me find peace."

I took the sugar packet and my fingers grazed his palm—a subtle thrum of electricity burned between us. *Did he feel it too?*

"Close your eyes," Emmanuel said, his voice deep and quiet. A child laughed nearby, and a mother shushed them. "Ask your question." His voice was so low I barely heard him.

I squeezed the sugar packet between my fingers feeling the individual grains. A burning desire roared in my gut to see Megan again, to see her eyes flash at me, a shared secret, a shared past. I wanted Megan back.

A tear slipped down my cheek, and I opened my eyes. I went to swipe at my face. "Wait," Emmanuel took the sugar packet from me and caught the tear as it fell off my chin. He moved the packet up and dabbed at my eyes, the paper wet against my skin. I closed my eyes and felt his breath on my cheek. "She'll like that," he said, handing me back the sugar packet.

"She likes tears?"

"Anything authentic," he answered. "Go ahead, put it on the crypt."

Reaching onto my tiptoes, I placed the packet between a bottle of rum and a piece of chewing gum on the roof's edge.

The desire burning in me—this deep need to see someone again—reminded me of losing my father.

We lived together in a wood cabin deep in an evergreen forest. The trees grew so thick that even on the sunniest days light could barely reach the forest floor.

It was just the two of us, and he never left me alone. Where Dad went, so did I—hunting, fishing, gathering wood. We did it all side by side.

I rode our mare, Honey, as my father walked beside us. An easy silence interrupted by the crunch of snow under foot. A rippling growl froze us. Before I saw the danger, father slapped Honey's rump so that she bolted toward home.

I looked back over my shoulder. A wolf leapt, latching onto Dad's shoulder, and knocking him to the ground.

I screamed.

Honey ran faster—my fear fueling hers. We went around a bend and I lost sight of Dad.

The mare slid to a stop, and I flopped over her neck, my balance off, my mind a mess. Honey reeled up. I fell back, landing in the snow, my hood flopping over my eyes.

I pushed back my coat to discover a wolf, hackles raised, blocking our path. Part of its muzzle looked like it had been gnawed off and its eyes glowed an eerie phosphorescent green.

Honey just stood there, trembling, her breath coming in frightened snorts. I'd never seen her like that before, frozen in place; it wasn't natural. The flight instinct should have taken over.

The wolf started forward, its mangled nose pulsing at the air. I grabbed at my bow to pull it around to the front of my body.

The wolf lunged.

I blocked it with my bow, keeping the creature's jaws inches from my face. Blood and saliva flew out of its mouth, landing cold and wet on my cheeks.

My biceps shook, the yellow and cracked teeth inching closer. My arms gave out, and the wolf fell upon my shoulder. Teeth ripped through my coat and dug into my flesh. I screamed as much from fear as pain.

An arrow pierced its eye, and the wolf collapsed, all of it's weight lying on top of me. I struggled out from under the body, crying and hyperventilating. My father stood twenty feet away, swaying. His left arm hung loose in its socket. His forearm and hand looked like tattered clothing. Blood dripped off them, staining the white snow.

In his right hand he held his bow. Two wolves ran behind him. I screamed, pointing, and my father turned, almost falling. I brought my bow up and, tears blurring my vision, fired at the approaching beasts. My arrow found its mark—one wolf fell into the deep snow.

The second wolf leaped onto him. I ran up, firing arrow after arrow into the creature's back, but it kept up its assault on my father's neck. Out of arrows, my father convulsing under the beast, I picked up a fallen branch and swung, putting all of my small weight behind the strike—knocking the wolf off and splintering the branch.

The wolf turned on me.

I held the sharp shard of wood in my hand. It launched itself at me, and I held *up the stake. Both of us fell to the ground, and the wood drove through the creature's throat, into its brain, killing it.*

Pinned under the wolf's weight, my teeth chattered with fear. I pushed the corpse off and crawled to my father. He lay in the snow, his eyes fluttering, blood caught in his beard and dappling his cheeks. I put my gloved hands over the wound at his neck.

"Darling," Emmanuel's voice brought me back to the present. He held out another sugar packet. They were the brown organic ones, and I pictured him slipping a few extra into his pocket when he got his coffee in the morning. *Had he thought of me then? Or did he always come here and offer sugar to this… spirit.*

I dabbed the fresh tears with the sugar packet. As I placed it on the edge of the crypt, my hunger rose; desire licked at my insides, building heat and anger. I had no questions, only requests. "Return her to me," I whispered.

Stepping back, I clasped my hands in front of me, lacing the fingers, and feeling the bones crush against each other as I squeezed. *I need to make the pain something I control.*

Tears rolled down my cheeks. Emmanuel didn't say anything; he just handed me a tissue. "Are you ready to go?" he asked gently.

I shook my head. "No, I want to stay for a minute. Go ahead."

"Are you sure?"

"Yes."

"Okay," he sounded unsure but Emmanuel didn't argue with me. "I'll see you at band practice."

I nodded, not looking over at him. He waited for another beat and then turned and left.

As the sky darkened, voices of other visitors faded. I sat down, my back against the mausoleum across from Suki's, my legs out in front, ankles crossed a foot away from the offerings lining the base of the crypt.

I didn't know why I wanted to stay but some instinct convinced me I'd find answers in this death filled place.

Street lights turned.

I thought about my father, about the final sounds he'd gurgled out, the way his eyes rolled into his head.

I pictured Megan's empty room and couldn't help the flicker of hope that burned in my chest. I didn't know for *sure* she was dead. Miracles happened.

A group passed outside the cemetery wall, laughing. I pulled out my phone, swiping it awake; the screen glowed.

"We call it the spark of life for a reason," said a voice. I turned quickly, my speed fueled by adrenaline, to see a woman standing in the lane. "Those screens will be the end of us," she continued as I scrambled to my feet, shoving my phone back into my purse.

The stranger wore a long white skirt and loose blouse with a wide lace collar. Her hair was wrapped in a scarf dotted with red needlepoint stars.

"Don't be afraid." She shuffled forward, her movements accompanied by a jingle. Bracelets on her wrists, gold, copper, and silver, all tinkled against each other. "Stay," she said. "You are here for a reason."

The woman stood in front of Suki's mausoleum with her back to me as she reached up to the roof's edge and placed a fresh candle there. She struck a match, the scratch of the sulfur head against the rough grain on the box tingled over my skin. *I love that sound.*

"I can help you," she said as she raised the match to the candle.

Her movement produced more jingles as she turned to me, holding something close to her side. It was partially hidden in the folds of her skirt, but I could see black feathers and a strand of beads hanging down. "What do you mean?" I asked her. "You can help me?"

"You're looking for your friend."

"What do you know about her?" My voice came out uneven, as I took a step forward.

The woman smiled, her teeth yellow in the candle's flickering glow. "I can find your friend." Her smile grew larger. "For a price."

"Of course," I shook my head, turning away, figuring she'd been listening in on Emmanuel and me. She was a fraud.

"Because I ask to be paid for my services, you think I'm a liar," she said to my back, her voice louder, edging on angry. "Do you play for free?"

I turned back to her. She was closer than I'd thought, almost touching me. "I don't know what your game is," I said. "But I'm not interested." She grabbed my bicep. "Hey!" I struggled to pull away, but her grip was like a vise.

"You don't want to find your friend anymore? Or are you afraid maybe she left you on purpose?"

I stopped struggling and looked into her dark and deep-set eyes. She held up a plume of black feathers tied to a chicken foot, the skin looking almost like scales. A string of red beads held the feather in place. "Pay me twenty and I will find your friend."

"How?"

She smiled, her teeth shiny. "Magic," she said as she let go of me, releasing a laugh that ricocheted off the surrounding gravestones, and bounced back in a strange and disconcerting echo.

She walked over to the Suki crypt and squatted in front of it, her long skirt bunching on the ground. Placing the chicken foot at the center of the makeshift shrine, she looked over her shoulder at me. "You pay in advance."

I hesitated for a moment. *I have nothing to lose but cash.*

I pulled a twenty out of my purse. There was one more in there, and it represented a larger portion of my total assets than I liked to admit. Bending forward, I passed it to her. She snatched the paper from my fingers, staying in a squat at the base of the mausoleum, not bothering to look at me.

The candle threw light around our corner of the cemetery, flickering against the old structures, making their cracks and shadows dance in the little flame's glow. Above us the clouds hung low, the lights from the city reflecting off them as a burgundy glow.

"Put down your things," she said. I placed my violin on the ground. "Your purse too." I put my small leather bag next to the case, hoping she wasn't about to knock me out and steal them both.

She began to chant, letting her head rock back and forth. Gray smoke that smelled of sage and something else, something slightly rotten, rose up in front of her.

She stood quickly, so fast that her bracelets didn't jingle different notes but released one tone. Setting the feathered chicken foot on top of the mausoleum, she chanted words I couldn't understand. She turned around, slowly, bringing the smoke with her.

The stranger raised her hands above her head, the bangles tinkling as they fell down her arms. There was a smudge stick in her left hand: tightly tied sage, one end of it bright embers with pale smoke billowing from it. With each step she took toward me, her voice and the clinking of her bracelets grew louder. Her eyes swiveled in their sockets, and she bowed from side to side, circling with the sage.

Raising her left foot, she bent her knee up to her waist and then slammed it down hard. She raised her right leg before crashing it down. Spittle flew from her mouth, the mist growing thicker as she danced in front of me, the sounds of beads and bracelets and chanting overwhelming. I pressed against the mausoleum behind me.

She stopped suddenly, falling to her knees, the white skirt puffing around her. Nodding her head forward, the woman kept her hands up in the air. The smoke poured from the smudge stick, backlit by the flames of the candle she'd left on the top of the crypt.

She lowered it to her breast, the fog clouding up over her, creating a thick curtain between us. I heard a sharp intake of breath, and then she tipped to the side and collapsed onto the cemetery lane. The smudge stick rolled to my feet, the smoke turning white as it tapped against my shoe.

The soft sizzle of burning sage was the only sound. "Hello?" My voice caught on the smoke and shifted into a cough. I kicked the smudge stick away, and it rolled down the path.

I coughed again as I bent over the woman. Her face was totally relaxed. She had a delicate nose, full lips, long eyelashes, and a sharp jawline. Lying still on the ground, she looked different; younger and gentler, pretty. Her eyes popped open, startling me. "You cannot see her again," she declared, her voice firm.

"What?" The wind changed, and vapor from the smudge stick blew over us.

She sat up and grabbed my shoulders, her fingers like claws, reminding me of the chicken foot. "You must stop looking for your friend."

"Do you know where she is?" I asked, my eyes burning, the smoke growing thicker.

"You cannot find her," The stranger's voice boomed, bouncing off the surrounding crypts.

I struggled free of her grasp, pushing into a standing position. "Tell me where she is! Tell me!"

Suddenly the stranger stood in front of me. I felt disoriented by the smoke. The flame from her candle seemed to glow brighter. "I'll pay you more." I turned to my purse, pulling out the other twenty dollar bill. Grasping it, I spun to her. The candle backlit the stranger. She seemed to be just a silhouette, a shadow I was begging for help.

"No!" Her voice boomed around me as if it came from every corner of the graveyard. "You must stop looking for her. She is dead but not gone. The most dangerous place to be. Do not join her!"

The flame flickered out, darkening the narrow space between the mausoleums. The money slipped from my fingers; a whoosh of air, and she disappeared. Grabbing for my purse, I found my phone and turned on the flashlight app. I aimed my beam of light at the altar. The candle and feathered chicken foot were gone. A mist of smoke, the strong incense of sage, and a hint of something rotten lingered.

Gathering up my fiddle and purse, I hurried out of the graveyard, my flashlight making the spaces between the graves seem that much darker, so I ran, fear creeping up my spine, raising hairs on the back of my neck.

CHAPTER FIVE

I BELIEVED the first ten years of my life were a hallucination. I have vivid, joyful memories of growing up with a loving father who cherished me and died to save me.

"Run, Darling. Run." With his final breaths, each word punctuated by a spray of blood, he told me to get home and climb into the bottom kitchen cabinet. *"Close the door, squeeze your eyes shut, and wait."*

I did exactly what he said.

I sprinted through the snow, my body covered in sweat, fear and grief warring inside of me.

I burst through the front door, the smell of our home hitting me: a mix of smoke scent and rosemary, the musk of wet dog, the aroma of antelope stew.

There were pots and pans in the cabinet my father told me to climb in. I tore them out, tossing them behind me—they clanged on the wooden floor. The only things I took in with me were our bows. My father's was almost twice the size of mine, which made sense because he was about twice the size of me. I pushed it in first, angling it so that it fit. Positioning myself next to it, I drew my bow tight to my chest. Light leaked in around the door, but when I closed my eyes, it was pitch black behind my lids.

That is how they found me; huddled in a kitchen cabinet with my eyes squeezed shut. But on the other side of that cabinet door wasn't the two-room cabin my father built. It was an apartment in a four-story building. I was in the most northern housing project in all of the United Tribes territory. I was in a different world.

Police discovered me when they responded to calls from the downstairs neighbors about a putrid leak in their bathroom. Apparently, my "real" father died a very different death than the one I'd imagined.

I remember the police officer who opened that cabinet door as clearly as my father's dying words. It is seamless, and yet, impossible.

When I told the social worker about who I was and how I got in there, she listened attentively, nodding her head and taking notes on a yellow legal pad. She reached across the interrogation table and covered my hands with hers. They were warm and rough. She smelled like sweet summer flowers, even though snow still covered the ground.

"Darling, sweetie, I'm sorry. You witnessed something horrible—"

"I know," I said.

She shook her head, her gold hoop earrings brushing against her cheeks. "That whole thing with the dogs, Darling—"

"They weren't dogs. They were wolves. Sick wolves that killed my father."

"None of that happened." I opened my mouth to speak but she forged ahead. "It's okay. I'm going to get you some medication that will help."

I took the pills but when Megan and I ran away, I didn't take them with me. And since I'd left the north behind I'd been fine. Until the incident in the cemetery. *Did I just hallucinate again? Is there any other explanation?*

I sprinted all the way home, and when I got through my front door, I slammed it shut and forced the deadbolt into place. My heart wanted to escape my body. *It will beat its way out.* My lungs burned.

I walked into the living room on unsteady legs. Dropping my violin and purse on the couch, I went to the kitchen and filled a glass with water, chugging it down, water leaking out the sides of my mouth. Some went down the wrong way and I coughed, sputtering.

My eyes filled with tears, and I looked down at my hands. My vision was blurred, and my lungs hurt as I struggled to gain my composure. *What is happening to me?* I swiped at my eyes, clearing them; refilling the glass, I passed back through my living room and opened my balcony doors to get some fresh air.

Megan had always dreamed of living in this neighborhood and having a balcony where we could grow a small garden. I stepped up to the railing. The narrow space was lined with plants, and the smell of them comforted me. The wind rustled and leaves bent and swayed, brushing against me.

I could feel the energy rising from the street below. Dinner hour was coming to an end, voices were growing louder, instruments were being tuned. Soon the neighborhood would fill with people, with revelers; music would blare, feet would stomp, and the heart of Crescent City would beat right below me.

It hadn't, before that moment, occurred to me to leave. But as I stood there looking down at the people milling beneath me, I realized I couldn't stay. Without Megan, I would be gripped by madness, again. I needed her back. Or I need to move on with my life.

Tendrils of pleasure rippled away from me—a stone dropped into the center of a still pond. Heat flickered over my body, flames starving for my flesh. *I do not fear them. I am of fire and light.*

He laughed against my neck, and it spiraled down my body. Tension built and unraveled, like a rope losing its form, until just a single thread remained, pulled taunt.

A slice of pain and the tension released. *Empty nothingness remains.*

Hunger flooded me. I tore at flesh, my jaw wide, the taste of blood on my tongue invigorating. Throwing back my head, I groaned with satisfaction. *Flesh fuels me.*

The dream shifted, and I found myself alone in the woods, again. A chilled mist spiraled around me as I turned, squinting into the veiled landscape. My nightshirt provided little protection against the cold, but I clutched it close as my teeth began chattering. I should run. But where?

A movement in the mist startled me—a creature close and circling closer. My body vibrated with the need to run. I gave in to it, sprinting through the darkness, hands out in front of me, batting away branches and glancing off trunks.

A root caught my foot and I flew forward, landing hard on the ground, something sharp cutting my hand. Ignoring the pain, I scrambled to my knees, grabbing at a bush—shaking loose cold water—but before I could find my feet, fingers gripped my hair and yanked me back.

The fresh pain brought tears to my eyes. A hard, muscled arm wrapped around my waist, forcing my back flush against a male body. My feet lifted off the ground. I kicked, meeting shins. A deep rumbling chuckle radiated from him to me.

"Let me go," I yelled.

"Oh, but I don't have you."

The fingers loosened in my hair. His arm slid around my neck and applied light pressure. I tried to twist away, but the forearm at my throat tightened. *Go limp.* But I couldn't. Some part of me couldn't give in. I fought harder, and the pressure increased. My chin tilted up as I opened my mouth and gasped for air, but there was nowhere for it to go.

The darkness of the forest closed in, spotting across my vision until it filled with pure black.

A pinpoint of light grew slowly as if walking toward the end of a tunnel. But I wasn't moving. I lay totally still, my heart beat thudding loudly in my ears as a pure, bright whiteness flooded my vision.

"Stop searching," a voice spoke in the void.

I tried to sit up, to gain some kind of traction on the space, but I couldn't move. *I can't move! It's a dream. Only a dream…*

Knocking sounded in the distance. "Give up," the voice said again as the white faded into grey. As I rose to consciousness, the knocking grew louder. I reached for my dream journal, the last wispy memories of another dream slipping away from me as a male voice called my name.

I pulled my robe on over the T-shirt and cotton shorts I'd slept in. "Coming," I snapped.

"About time," the man responded—it was Michael. *What's he doing here?* I didn't think I could take getting reamed again. But when I opened the door, he was grinning and holding a beer; Emmanuel stood next to him, a subtle smile curling his lips.

"Hey," I said.

"You're still sleeping?" Michael ran his eyes over my body, taking in the stained robe. He smiled. "It's two in the afternoon."

I leaned against the doorjamb. "What can I do for you boys?" I asked.

"Get dressed and run a brush through your hair, girl; it's making up for being an asshole day," Michael said. Emmanuel cleared his throat, and Michael looked over at him. Emmanuel raised his eyebrows, and Michael sighed. "Also," he said, turning back to me. "I'm sorry." He cast his gaze to his feet. "I didn't mean to be so hard on you." Michael glanced up to see how his apology was landing. "Like, I said, I'm an asshole."

"Thanks," I replied, feeling my throat constrict, tears filling my eyes. *Way to get over emotional.* "Come in," I offered, gesturing into the apartment before I lost it.

"Great place," Michael said, looking around the living room; it opened into the kitchen, with the old-fashioned pocket doors pushed aside.

"Thanks, I'll be out in a minute."

Leaving them lounging on the couch, sipping their beers, I went into my bedroom and dressed quickly—a pair of jeans and a white T-shirt. After brushing my hair, I braided it into two plaits, then wrapped them up around my head and secured them in the back with a couple of bobby pins. Sitting on my bed, I buckled on a pair of leather sandals. I pulled my comforter over my pillows before checking myself in the mirror.

My cheeks were flushed, and I appeared almost fevered. Hunger gnawed at me as I examined my reflection. I decided to change tops because the V-neck of the white shirt was too much. I put on a sports bra and a dark blue button-down blouse with yellow bunnies on it. The buttons strained to contain my chest. Despite my conservative outfit and sweetly braided hair, I still looked wanton. That's what my foster father would have called it. I shook my head, blocking him from my memory.

Both of the men stood as I came out. "You look nice," Michael said with a smile.

"Thanks." He was obviously trying to make me feel good, and I appreciated the effort.

"Yes, beautiful," Emmanuel said, his voice quiet. I looked over at him, and he held my gaze. The way his eyes lingered on me made my throat constrict. *I'm starving.*

"Where we headed?" I asked, crossing to the kitchen and filling a cup with water.

Michael followed me. "There's a parade a friend of mine is in. Should be fun."

I gulped down the water and left the empty glass by the sink. "Okay," I said, turning to Michael with a smile. *Clearly, I've lost my mind, why not join a parade?*

CHAPTER SIX

As WE LOCKED up our bikes, I checked out the small group gathering for the parade. "Not a big showing," I said, eyeing the smattering of people outside of the bar—mostly men, what Megan called "green meanies". Green because they were so dirty that their skin and clothing seemed to take on a brown-green tinge. Mean because they got in your face if you didn't give them money when they begged on the street.

Megan and I played on the streets when we first arrived—I've never worked so hard as that first year in Crescent City. It pissed Megan off when the "green meanies" begged for money without offering anything back.

"Don't worry, more will join us on the route," Michael said. "People with day jobs don't get off for a while." He came up next to me and offered me a beer.

I took it and popped the can open. Michael threw his arm across my shoulders. His scent, a mix of sweat from our ride and beer from his breath, swirled around me. His touch warmed my back. That strange hunger clawed at my insides. *I'm so empty.*

"Hey, Michael?" Emmanuel said from over by his bike. "This lock you loaned me is stuck again."

Michael sighed and smiled, giving my shoulder a squeeze before releasing me to go and help Emmanuel. I took a long slug off the beer, trying to shake that empty sensation.

"Come on," Michael said once Emmanuel's lock was secured. "We have time for a shot before the parade begins." He led the way to the bar, a single-story building with a door that swung both ways and tinted windows filled with neon signs for liquor brands.

A tingling of awareness raised the hairs on the back of my neck. I turned, my eyes drawn to the shadow under a balcony. A man stood in the doorway, the pale blue of his eyes shining in the darkness. *The stranger from the hospital?* Hunger struck me like an anvil hitting hot metal, and I stumbled, twisted by the strength of it.

Emmanuel caught my arm, keeping me from falling on my ass. *Super cool, that's me.* When I looked back the man was gone. *Did I hallucinate him? Craptastic.*

"Are you hungry?" Emmanuel asked, leading me into the dark bar— it smelled of stale cigarettes and spilled beer.

"I could eat." *Understatement much.*

I glanced up at Emmanuel—his eyes with their long lashes flashed purple in the dim space. His shoulders, broad but not bulky, made my mouth water. I dropped my gaze to his hands...shivers of savage want ran down my spine. *Starving is more like it.*

"How about a slice of pizza? I'll go grab you one. There is a pretty good place down the block," Emmanuel offered.

"Pizza?" Michael said. "The breakfast of champions. I'll take a slice too. Thanks, man."

Emmanuel smiled down at me. "My pleasure." His voice felt like a physical thing, a rough presence rumbling over my skin. "I'll be right back."

Michael ordered three shots and another round of beer. "But mine's still full," I said.

"Finish it up then," Michael countered. He leaned against the bar, his T-shirt rising up and showing off his obliques, the muscles defined and skin silky smooth. The hunger churned into nausea. Michael pushed the shot in front of me. "A toast," he said, holding up his own glass. "To our band."

I picked up the glass and clinked it against his. "Yes," I said. "To the band."

He downed the drink in one go. I tried to follow suit but could only swallow half. My eyes burned, and I coughed. "You're all right," Michael said and waved the bartender over for another round.

By the time Emmanuel returned with our slices, I was one and a half shots in. I devoured the cheese pizza without really tasting it. "Here," Michael said, pushing two shots toward Emmanuel. "You've got to catch up." Then he bit into his slice, grease escaping down his chin.

Emmanuel handed him a napkin and then gave one to me. I wiped at my face. *Super cool, take two.* Placing the crust on the paper plate, I resisted finishing it off in two quick bites.

By the time the brass band arrived, I was officially drunk. "Come on." Michael tried to take my hand, but Emmanuel distracted him by passing him the bill.

"Here." I pulled out my wallet, then remembered I didn't have any money since I'd spent it all at the cemetery. That made me laugh, and both boys turned to look at me. "Sorry." I suppressed my smile.

"Please don't apologize for laughing," Emmanuel said.

"Yeah, it's nice," Michael said. "Just what you need. Don't worry about the tab," Michael continued. "It's my treat. I'm making up for being an asshole, remember?"

"Thanks." I shoved my wallet back in my purse.

A loud trumpet sounded, and Michael looked up from counting money, a smile on his face. He dropped the cash and grinned at us as he turned for the door.

I squinted against the setting sun as we walked back outside. Michael was chatting with a guy wearing a tuba; it wrapped around his body like a thick, gold snake. The tuba player laughed at something Michael said.

"Everyone likes him," I said to Emmanuel. "Don't they?"

He glanced at Michael. "Sure. He's charming, good-looking, talented. What's not to like?"

I smiled, the shots and beer making me feel loose and brave. "Sometimes he's mean," I responded.

"Sorry," he said.

"I deserve it," I admitted. "I've been sucking."

"You'll get it back," Emmanuel said. "You've just got to let the music in again." He put a hand on my shoulder—warm and heavy and oh so nice. "And Darling, no one should be mean to you. Ever."

I stared at his lips, my body buzzing. My eyes rose to meet his. "Sometimes when I'm talking to you, when your hair falls over your face like that, and you're looking down at me, I feel like no one else can see us." *Did I just say that out loud? Egads. I'm a dork of the first magnitude.*

Emmanuel's eyes brightened, and a soft smile stole over his mouth. "Me too." His voice was a whisper. A grin broke across my face as the band began to play a marching song I recognized from other parades. "Come on," he said, gesturing with his chin for us to move with the music.

We all danced down the block—the green meanies, a new collection of girls in short skirts, a family that looked like they might be tourists, two drag queens with a cadre of fans, a man on one of those antique bicycles with the giant front wheel, and the three of us.

The beers and shots in my system ran roughshod over the pizza, and I danced with the rest of the crowd, throwing my hands over my head, feeling the beat, like a second heartbeat, as if it was a part of me, something that could not be ignored.

Michael passed me another beer, the tab already popped. Emmanuel pulled a flask from his pocket and tipped his head back, drinking it in. I reached out for the flask, and he gave me a crooked smile before handing it over.

Smoky and hot, the liquor burned my mouth and raged down my throat. Handing it back, I did a spin, and danced forward.

As the sun slipped below the horizon, two old ladies, with big smiles that pushed their cheeks up, making their eyes mere slits, came down their front steps holding their skirts in their hands, swishing them back and forth, reminding everyone that life ain't over till you're dead.

Young men wearing tank tops exposing their strong shoulders and long shorts hanging low on their hips, held the edges of their ball caps and moved their feet in ways that seemed impossible to me. Watching one, I bounced against Michael; he wrapped his arm around my waist, pulling me against him.

A heat coursed between us, and hunger rose in my throat, my mouth going dry. He grinned down at me, the soft tone of dusk lighting him just right. His hand squeezed my hip, and he began to bend his head down toward me—as if drawn by some unseen force. Fear gripped me and I jerked my head away from him. The hunger tried to pull me back to him but I spotted Emmanuel and it settled at the sight of him

He was frowning at a woman watching the parade from her porch. She was big—not just tall but also carrying an extra fifty pounds or so. Her breasts were barely contained by the black, low-cut T-shirt she wore.

She was dancing…in a way. Her feet bare, she shuffled down to the street. The whites of her eyes were clearly visible. There was so much gel in her black hair that it looked wet.

Emmanuel glanced over at me. His eyes traveled to Michael's hand on my hip and his frown deepened. Michael let me go easily when I pulled away. He continued to dance forward, moving with the crowd.

"Everything okay?" I asked Emmanuel when I reached him.

"Yes." Emmanuel glanced over his shoulder at the odd woman, again. She'd joined the parade now.

"She looks really high," I said to him.

He bit his lip and nodded. "Sure." Then he smiled at me and brought his flask out from his back pocket. "Let's dance," he said. I nodded, and we caught up to Michael, who was chatting up one of the girls in short skirts.

I took another swig off Emmanuel's flask, thinking I tasted something herbal in it this time. "What is this?" I asked.

But Emmanuel didn't answer; he was looking behind us. I followed his gaze. The high woman moved quickly through the crowd, headed straight for the band. Emmanuel took my hand and pulled me to the edge of the parade as she barreled through the center. "Maybe we should go," he said.

"What?" Michael whined at him. "No way! The sun just set."

Emmanuel's attention stayed focused on the high woman. She came up behind the trumpet player and raised her right leg high, then crashed it down, her bare foot smacking against the pavement. She raised her left leg and did the same. Letting her head roll on her neck she reached out and grasped at the air. I noticed that the side of her neck looked weird. I squinted through the crowd.

"Is she hurt?" I asked.

"Shit," Emmanuel said. "We need to go."

He took my arm and pulled, but I was rooted to the spot, watching her head loll. *Are those her tendons I'm seeing?*

She reached out and grabbed the trumpet player's shoulders.

He tried to shrug her off, his hat falling askew, but she yanked him toward her mouth. He stopped playing and started to turn.

She bit down hard onto his cheek.

The man screamed and the music fell apart, stuttering to a stop. The crowd's gyrations slowed and stopped with the music, their attention drawn to the attack taking place.

High Woman held the trumpet player tight to her chest. He fought back, striking with his instrument and his fist. A young man pulled a gun from the waistband of his low-slung shorts and held it on the woman. "Let him go!" he yelled.

Screams rose. Heels clattered on the pavement.

Emmanuel pulled on me harder but I didn't move—I couldn't. My brain struggled to digest the events in front of me, incapable of doing anything else... including running for my life. There was something horrifyingly familiar about the whole scene.

The gun fired and I jerked at the sound. The bullet entered High Woman's stomach. She didn't let go.

The second shot hit her in the back. Chunks of flesh and blood splattered across the sidewalk. She ignored the new wound and stepped into the trumpet player, knocking him to the ground, falling with him.

Lying on top of him, his trumpet now crushed between them, his arms trapped, legs weighted by her, she reared her head back and drove her teeth into his neck, cutting off a fresh scream.

Emmanuel pulled at me, but I shook my head. The gunman stood over High Woman and unloaded the rest of his clip into her back but she kept biting, the trumpet player's body shaking beneath her.

Emmanuel scooped me up into his arms and ran down the block, holding me tight. I could smell the mix of beer and smoky herbs on his breath. I placed my hand against his chest and felt Emmanuel's heart. It seemed to pulse into my hand, each beat throbbing through me. Even more powerful than the rhythm of the music from the parade. And just as fragile...

CHAPTER SEVEN

EMMANUEL LOWERED ME ONTO A COUCH. I sank into the cushions, and he slipped his arms from beneath me. Even without his body against mine, I felt his heartbeat thrumming through me. "What the fuck was that?" Michael yelled as he paced back and forth. I couldn't have said it better myself.

Emmanuel sat in an armchair next to me, his elbows on his knees. "Are you hurt?" he asked, his eyes intent.

"No," My voice vibrated with the strange energy coursing through me.

Michael stomped over to Emmanuel. "Dude, what the fuck was that?" he yelled again.

Emmanuel looked up at him. "What do you think it was?"

Michael turned and paced away. Emmanuel leaned back in his chair and pulled his flask out of his front pocket. His Adam's apple bobbed as he drank deeply from the small container. Michael came back over and stood impatiently above him until Emmanuel handed it over.

He took a long swig and then turned to me. "What do you think it was?"

I swallowed, my head fuzzy. *I feel so strange.* "I heard there was a drug causing attacks like that."

"What drug?" Michael asked.

Emmanuel's eyes searched my face. "It's been on the news," I said. "It causes terrible hallucinations, and there was that attack last week."

"What attack?" Michael stepped closer to me.

I shrugged, uncomfortable under his angry scrutiny. "Didn't you hear about it?"

"Obviously not!" he yelled. "If I had, I wouldn't be fucking asking you about it, would I?"

"Ease up," Emmanuel said, his voice low and calm.

Michael took a deep breath, closed his eyes, and let it out slowly. "I'm sorry." His voice was tight. "Please, tell me about it." Michael's fists clenched and unclenched by his side.

"I don't know all the details, but a woman attacked a group of friends on their way home from the bar. They experienced seizures afterward and were brought to Mercy Hospital."

"Fuck." Michael turned away from me and took another sip from the flask.

I felt Emmanuel's gaze and turned to him. "I think you should stay here tonight," he said.

"Here?" I looked around for the first time. I was on a worn couch, under a high ceiling crossed with wooden beams. Across the large room was an open kitchen, the sink filled with dishes. Behind me a row of factory windows, two sheets crisscrossing them, neither large enough to cover the expanse alone, covered the wall.

"You can have my room," Emmanuel said. "Just stay until tomorrow." He put his hand over mine, and I could *feel* the steady beat of his heart again. *Why can I feel his pulse? What is happening?*

"I have to go to the hospital in the morning," I stared down at our hands. His thumb ran along mine, sending shivers over me.

"You shouldn't go to the hospital." His voice was smooth and soothing. *I want to agree with him.*

"No." I shook my head, trying to free myself from these odd sensations. "I have to. I'm needed. I'm donating bone marrow."

"What?" Michael stormed back over. "We have band practice all week. The Bell House Show is coming up." He referred to the booking our manager had made. She assured us that it would turn into a record contract. She was getting all the right people there.

"I know. I'll be fine."

"After a bone marrow transplant?"

"It's a harvest, not a transplant. Don't worry," I said, my voice lowering. "I've done it before. I'll be fine."

Michael huffed a laugh and paced away again.

"Please stay here," Emmanuel said. "I'm not comfortable with you going home alone, and I don't even think it's safe to escort you."

"It's that bad?" I asked.

"Why risk it? The cops are probably freaking out. Not to mention the face-eating junkies." As if to prove his point, a siren began to wail in the distance.

"Okay," I answered, nodding my head. He smiled and removed his hand from mine. The steady beat of his heart left with his touch. *So strange.*

Michael collapsed onto the couch next to me and his hand grazed my bare arm.

It felt like a deep cut, the kind where you don't feel pain, just the jolt of cold metal slicing through flesh.

I breathed him in, a thrum rising into a crescendo.

Suddenly Michael's lips pressed to mine and our tongues met in a desperate dance. A hand pulled at my shirt, another gripped my braids. Stubble grated against my chin, a palm found my breast, heat poured between us.

Strong hands yanked me back. I was straddling Michael. *What the hell?* He still clutched my hair, refusing to release me. Emmanuel roared and brought his arm down onto Michael's wrist—it made a sickening crack. Michael's fingers fell away, and he cradled the injured arm to his chest—skin gray and eyes sunken.

Emmanuel dragged me across the room. I fought him, my throat dry, body buzzing, hunger coursing through me. *I need to continue that kiss. Keep taking! I'll never be sated.*

A pang of pure revulsion racked through me—an avalanche of shame and fear rolled after the wave of lust. I gagged, my body convulsing against Emmanuel's arms.

His hold softened, and I dropped to my knees, staring down at the wooden floor, the knots of color, and the heads of nails, my vision pulsing, blurred by tears.

My hair hung around me in strands, some of it still up, the rest of it torn loose, shielding me from the room. Slowly my breathing returned to normal. I sat back on my heels and looked up.

Emmanuel was standing over Michael, his hands on the lead singer's wrist. "What's happening?" Michael asked.

"Everything is fine," Emmanuel said as he released Michael's arm, laying it gently on his chest. "I think we've all had a little too much to drink. Let's go to bed."

A shudder ran through me. It felt amazing. *What the what is happening?* Fear chilled the heat inside me. *Did someone drug me?* I focused on the two men in front of me—that wild need tearing at my insides. "Did you put something in my drink?" I asked, my voice choked.

"What?" Emmanuel turned to me. "No," he shook his head, his curls bouncing. "Of course not." He sounded insulted. *I did just accuse him of drugging me.* But how else could this be explained?

"What about Michael?" I asked. *I want to kiss him until he dies.* I shuddered at the errant, terrifying thought.

"No, we've all had a lot to drink. And we saw something horrible." Emmanuel crossed the room to me. "Come on, I'll take you to bed. It's been a rough day for everyone."

He didn't touch me, just stood over me, his hand out… offering to help. "I don't feel right."

"You can stay in my room," Emmanuel offered. "You can lock yourself in, Okay?" I didn't answer him. "I won't touch you," he promised.

But that's not what I want at all.

I woke up with a start, the room at once familiar and foreign. A dream curled at the edge of my mind, but when I grabbed for it the memories dissipated like thin clouds on a windy day. I flopped back on the pillow, huffing with frustration.

Despite the high ceilings and half-shrouded factory windows, there was something about Emmanuel's space that felt right, almost like a sanctuary. It even smelled like incense.

Votive candles lined the windowsill, their unlit wicks standing out as black silhouettes against the light coming through the white sheets covering the window. Pushing the comforter away, I slipped out of the big bed.

I wore a T-shirt that smelled like Emmanuel. The hem brushed my thighs, closer to my knees than hips. My ankle-length white socks quieted my footsteps as I crossed to the windows.

Wax covered the sill and dripped onto the rough wooden floor below. The fresh candles' bases had melted directly into the old ones. Black, blue, purple, and red twisted around each other like streams of water running down the side of a mountain.

I traced my finger over the smooth surface and felt an energy lingering there. *The spark of life.* That was the first thing the woman I'd seen in the cemetery said to me. What did she mean?

A car drove by, making the shadows from the draped sheets race across the ceiling. Cool air caressed my skin, and I sensed the lingering movement in the solidified wax, could almost taste the fumes from the passing vehicle. *Someone must have put something in my beer.*

But that didn't explain the strange woman in the cemetery. Maybe she was real. She said Megan was dead but not gone—and that rang true to me. I'd never felt that she was dead. Something tickled at the back of my mind. But as I tried to grasp onto it, the thought dissipated, like smoke, drifting away into the ether. *As elusive as the damn dreams.*

Dead but not gone…was Megan a ghost? Was the woman in the cemetery some kind of witchcraft? You couldn't live in Crescent City without hearing stories about spirits and other unknown dark things that go bump in the night. Maybe it wasn't a hallucination. Maybe none of it was.

I turned away from Emmanuel's candles.

Taking a fortifying breath I slide the deadbolt back and left the bedroom. Ambient light from the street lamps spilled into the kitchen. I padded forward, past the white cabinets flecked with grease near the stove, the full sink of dishes, and the counters littered with debris.

Emmanuel slept on the couch, his forearm across his eyes, blocking the light that came through the windows. I crouched down next to him, suddenly fascinated by the pulse I could see in his neck, just under the surface of his skin. I wanted to touch him, to lay my fingers there and feel his life pumping through him.

He woke with a start, and I fell back onto my butt. "Darling?" he said, his eyes shadowed in the dark room. I scrambled back to my feet. "What is it?" he asked.

I didn't answer for a moment, feeling like he'd caught me watching him...which he had. But I'd come out for a reason. "Did you—?" The sentence fell short, sounding too ridiculous.

"What?" He sat up, the blanket falling away from his bare chest. I turned away, unable to look at him. The brief glimpse of his sculpted body had sent electric currents of hunger through my gut and up my throat. "What's going on?" he asked. I glanced back at him furtively. He was rubbing at his head, mashing the curls around.

"That woman in the cemetery?"

"Darling, what are you talking about?" I couldn't read his expression in the darkness. "Here." He pulled his feet up, making room for me on the couch. "Sit." I stared at the space he'd made for me—so close to him. I sat down gingerly, keeping my feet on the floor, ready to run, not sure why I'd need to but ready none the less. "What happened in the cemetery?" he asked.

"You took me there." I stole a glance at him—the blanket pooled on his crossed leg, his sculpted shoulders hunched forward, his long-fingered hands resting in his lap.

"It's not an unusual place to go when you're looking for help. As shown by the number of question marks on that mausoleum."

"So...you don't know anything about her?"

He leaned back and pushed his hair behind his ears—trying to control the curls. "I thought she might come to you."

Hope bloomed in my chest. "Who?" it came out a whisper.

"Suki."

"So you've seen her?" I asked. He nodded. "What is she?" If she wasn't a hallucination, then maybe I could find Megan. If he'd seen this Suki too, then I wasn't crazy. My heartbeat quickened at the thought.

He shrugged. "Suki is powerful and old."

"A witch?" He nodded with a shrug. "She told me Megan was dead but not gone," I said.

Emmanuel's body tensed. "She did?"

"What does it mean? Dead but not gone?"

"I'm not sure." He bit his lip in thought, and it did something to me. Something that hurt *and* felt good. *What in the freaking what is going on?*

"Are you lying to me?" I asked, my confusion edged with anger. *There must be an explanation for all this!*

"Never." He met my gaze, his eyes shining in the half light. I had a strong urge to climb on top of him and capture those supple lips, feel that coarse stubble scratch my skin.

I swallowed; it sounded loud in the quiet room. Fear and desire swirled in my stomach as I resisted the pressing need to *take* him.

If I stay here one more second I'll kiss him. I'll humiliate myself. I'll hurt him.

I stood so quickly that I almost tipped over. "I better get back to bed." I rushed back to his room, not giving Emmanuel a chance to respond.

Pushing the deadbolt into place, I rested my forehead against the door.

Emmanuel has seen the woman in the cemetery too. She isn't a hallucination. Relief coursed through me even as that strange, powerful hunger beat at my chest.

CHAPTER EIGHT

I DIDN'T WANT to take off Emmanuel's shirt—the soft cotton, the bigness of it, how it hid me underneath—it made me feel safe.

"We must have all been drugged." Michael's hand slapped the table, shaking the coffee in our cups. "It's the only thing that makes sense." He nodded. "It's out of our systems now." He glanced at me and then quickly stood and paced to the coffee maker, refilling his almost full cup. "What we need to do is just concentrate on the music."

That humming was still there, though not as strong...but the memory of that kiss last night with Michael...the way I went after him. *Like a pilgrim wandering the desert and finally finding water...*

"I agree," I said, keeping my eyes on my coffee. "We should just forget the whole thing and concentrate on the music."

Emmanuel offered me a ride home—he drove a pickup truck with rust along its fenders and a rattle to its ride. We stopped by the bar and he put my bike in the bed. When we got to my place, Emmanuel carried it up the stairs for me.

"Thanks," I said at my door. "I'll see you at practice tomorrow."

"I'll take you to the hospital." He didn't say it like he was offering— more like he was *telling* me what was going to happen.

"I'll be fine."

Emmanuel stepped close to me, and a shiver ran down my spine. "Please," he said, his voice all soft and melty.

Why refuse him? Some idea of pride—that I can do everything on my own.

"Thanks, I just need a few minutes to get myself together. You can wait in the living room." I didn't look up at him, just turned my back to open the door, feeling the heat of him right behind me.

I showered and put on sweatpants and one of my own T-shirts. When I came out, Emmanuel stood. "Here," I said, holding out his shirt. "Thanks for letting me borrow it."

"Of course." He took the shirt, seeming to avoid touching me in the process.

We drove the short distance to the hospital. Emmanuel stopped in front of the main entrance and put the old truck into park. "I'll meet you up there," he said.

"You don't need to do that, really. I'll be fine."

"They don't like people to be alone after this kind of thing."

"I don't suffer from a lot of the side effects."

He met my gaze and bit down on his lip. I started to lean toward him —as if a magnet drew me. Then he broke eye contact. Turning forward, he nodded. "Sure," he said. "I'll see you at band practice tomorrow?"

"Yeah," I said, my lips dry, throat aching.

I opened the door, but Emmanuel grabbed my hand before I could get out. That zing of electricity was there, but felt more like pins and needles than a live wire, now. I wondered how long it would take for the drugs to totally leave my system. "Darling," Emmanuel said when I didn't look at him.

"Yeah?"

"Call me if you need anything."

"Okay." I pulled away. The door creaked when I slammed it shut. As I went around in the revolving door, I looked back over my shoulder. Emmanuel's eyes found mine—a sudden, almost painful surge of electric current seemed to leap between us. The door kept going and I went with it, breaking the link between us. I stepped into the hospital lobby, breathless and lightheaded. Whatever they dosed us with was one hell of a drug.

I was in a dark crevice with just a slit of light above me. Floating toward it, I felt a sense of peace. I blinked at the bright light and saw a figure standing over me. My mouth was dry, and I swallowed. It seemed more difficult than it needed to be. I blinked again, and a halo of golden red hair blurred almost into focus…it was so familiar…

"Megan?" I strained to open my eyes. There was nothing but fluorescent tubes of light above me. Struggling with a woozy head and weak arms, I pushed myself into a sitting position. I was in a long hallway, my gurney pushed off to the side. A doctor and nurse I didn't recognize walked by, their heads down, conferring with each other.

Effervescent red hair bounced through a door at the end of the hall. "Megan!" I tried to yell, but only a croak came out. Pulling the thin blankets off me, I swung my legs to the side of the gurney and lowered my feet to the floor. It was laminated and cold against my bare toes. "Megan," I called again, using the gurney to push myself into a standing position.

"Darling, you shouldn't be up," I heard behind me, but I stepped toward the door. My legs were soft and unsure; I stumbled a step forward and clutched onto the gurney to keep from falling. A hand touched my shoulder. I wheeled around, flailing out at the person trying to stop me. It was Dr. Tor. He took a step back to avoid my attempted blow, his hands up. "Darling, you need to lie down."

My vision darkened at the edges, keeping the doctor at the center of a pinpoint. I turned back to chase Megan, determination strong in my gut. I felt a tug on my arm and looked down to see the needle in my IV straining to break loose. I ripped it out, a small spurt of blood shooting from the wound.

"Darling." It was the doctor again; he was in front of me. "You need to lie down." I tried to push past him but ended up just kind of falling onto him. He held me up, his arms around my waist, warm fingers on my naked back.

"No," I said. It came out hoarse and low, barely a protest.

"Darling, please," he said, his voice close to me, breath touching my cheek.

I wrenched free, falling backward, landing on my butt. The floor felt

cold and wet against my bare skin. Suddenly a nurse I recognized—
Harriet with the small scar—was by my side. "Darling, what are you
doing?" she asked, crouching next to me.

"Megan," I said.

Her face fell into a deep frown that conveyed sympathy and disap-
pointment in one sad expression. "Megan's gone, sweetheart. I'm sorry,
but she's not coming back."

The edges of my vision darkened again, slowly closing on the nurse's
lips, bare and honest. "No," I whispered before I slipped back into that
dark crevice.

Sun slanted through a window to my left, covering my body in a warm
glow. I was in a hospital bed this time, a blanket and sheet tucked around
me. The IV was gone, and the news played on a TV in the upper left
corner.

"You're awake," a voice said. I turned to find I had a roommate: an
older white guy, his mustache yellow, an oxygen feeder resting on it. He
wore the same gown I did. It was loose around his shoulders, gray hairs
sprouted from his chest and back, reaching toward his face.

"Yes," I said, my voice cracked. My side table held the ubiquitous
yellow cup with its straw. When I reached out for it, I groaned. *Everything
hurt.* The memory of falling in the hallway came flashing back to me.
Embarrassment chased on the memory's heels.

I made a fool of myself.

I'd always woken up feeling fine. What was different this time? A
shiver passed over me as I remember Megan leaning over me. *A hallucination? Or a reason to hope?*

"Can you believe this?" the man said, pointing at the TV. "That guy
who survived the crazy druggie attack? He got killed right here in this
hospital."

"He did?" I looked up to the TV, where a news anchor stood in front
of the hospital.

"Yeah, aren't you listening to me? Someone stabbed him through the
eye," he said.

"Oh."

"Don't you realize what this means?" He leaned on the bedrail, the oxygen tube straining against his upper lip. "It's starting."

"All right, that's enough of that, Mr. Combers," a nurse said as she walked through the door.

He looked over at her. "You're on the front lines," he told her. "By the time it really gets going, I'll probably be dead." The nurse pulled the curtain between our beds. "The end!" he yelled through the curtain. "The end is coming!"

"All right, Mr. Combers," she said again, placing her fists on her ample hips. "That's enough."

A half-hearted grumble was the only response. She turned her attention to me and smiled. "How are you feeling?"

"Sore," I said with a smile. "And embarrassed."

She waved a hand at me. "Oh, sweetheart, don't worry about it. Everyone is affected differently."

"That's never happened to me before—I've always come out of it feeling fine."

I knew in the logical part of my brain it was impossible for Megan to be bending over me, her hair rich and lush like before she got sick, but in my heart I wanted to believe. *Maybe it wasn't a hallucination.*

"Things change," the nurse said. "Dr. Tor wants to keep you another night." She picked up the blood pressure cuff next to my bed and reached for me.

I shook my head. "No, I'm going home," I said. *I can't stay here.*

"You're going to sign out against doctor's orders?" She pumped the cuff with one hand and put her stethoscope into her ears with the other, brows arched in disapproval.

"Yes," I said. She listened to my heart and looked at her watch. I waited until she released the pressure on the cuff. "Where are my clothes?" I asked. She sighed but gave them to me. I dressed quickly and checked myself out. Rushing onto the elevator, I felt a swell of relief that I'd gotten out of there. I wasn't sure why, but I knew I *had* to go.

CHAPTER NINE

THAT NIGHT I warred with my sheets. The dreams that had taunted me since Megan's disappearance played over and over—and I always woke before I got what I needed. Before I understood what was going on!

One minute I was burning hot, throwing my blankets to the side, and the next chilled to the bone and pulling the covers up to my neck, sometimes even dipping my head under the folds.

"Be careful." Megan's voice spoke so close I felt her breath on my ear. My eyes popped open, and I yanked the bedding away.

I was alone.

The window stood ajar, the curtains shifting in a breeze. Adrenaline hammered through my veins. *Just another dream.*

I crossed the room and looked out onto the back courtyard. The sun peeked over the buildings, casting a gray-pink glow on the space below. A cat bolted into the middle of the courtyard, skittering to a stop and turning back to the shadows. The feline bared its teeth and hissed at an unseen opponent.

A figure stepped to the edge of the shadow and I squinted through the hazy light of dawn trying to see them better. Blue eyes flashed in the darkness up at me. *The man I saw at the hospital and the parade.*

The cat skittered away.

The stranger stared up at me—his eyes the blue of ice *and* of flame. I leaned into the window, my hands gripping the frame. A wind swept the curtains in front of me, billowing them out the window, and when they fell again he was gone.

Humid air wrapped around me, and I swallowed, my throat dry and aching. *Who the hell is that?* I wasn't dreaming. That guy was real.

Sleep never came again and around noon, I went out to my balcony and stood looking down at the street. Two musicians played on the corner, the notes from their string instruments blending with their voices. People walked in pairs and small groups. Laughter and bright conversation interplayed with the song.

Over the course of Megan's illness, I'd become hyperaware of my cellphone, knowing that a call could come from the hospital at any moment. So when I heard the phone vibrating where I'd left it with my keys, I hurried inside to answer it.

"Darling Price, this is Dr. Issa Tor."

"Hi." My mind leaped to being half-naked on the floor, Dr. Tor trying to help me stand. Heat swept over my body. *Such a fool!*

"I was calling to check on you."

"I'm good," I said, brightening my voice so he would believe me.

"No swelling, flu-like symptoms? You're sleeping okay? Eating?"

"I'm fine," I said again. "How is the patient?"

"She's doing great," he said, his voice soft. "You probably saved her life."

Tears welled in my eyes, and a lump formed in my throat. *I couldn't save Megan, but I did help others.* It felt good. "I just provided the raw materials, but thank you."

"Without 'raw materials' like yours I'd be lost." I couldn't help but hiccup a small laugh. "Do you have anyone looking after you?"

I looked around my empty living room. "Yes," I lied.

"Your boyfriend? I saw him drop you off."

"He's my bandmate." I said it for myself as much as for Issa, so I'd remember it the next time I thought about Emmanuel's heartbeat vibrating through my entire body.

"Oh." Issa sounded disappointed. "So who is looking after you?"

"Someone else," I lied.

"Okay," he said, his tone unsure. "How did you sleep?"

"I'm fine," I said again.

"Please, Darling."

The word please surprised me. Out of all the doctors Megan and I dealt with, I couldn't remember any of them saying please. Especially not like that. "Please what?" I asked.

I could hear him breathing. "I'd like to come check on you. Would that be okay?"

"You want to come to my house?"

"I don't think you slept well last night. I think your body is hurting. I think you're in need of..." His voice faded for a moment but then he continued. "I want to check on you. Please."

It was the "please" that got me. I gave him the address.

His quiet but firm knock woke me thirty minutes later. *I don't remember falling asleep.* I wobbled on unsteady legs to the door. The smell of Chinese food wafted in when I opened it. Issa held up a brown paper bag. "Wonton soup," he said.

The door was the only thing holding me up. "Come in." My voice sounded weak and soft.

Issa stepped in, and I went to close the door, but instead I found myself falling with it and stumbling forward. Issa's hand shot out and caught my elbow. "Thank you." I tried to get my feet under me. "I'm fine," I said, even as the edges of my vision darkened.

I began to slide down the closed door. The paper bag of food thunked to the floor. Issa's hands pulled me up, wrapping me in an embrace. His face was right above mine. His eyes were sharp, looking at me hard. *I'm so hungry I could die.*

He picked me up, one arm under my knees, the other cradling my shoulders. My head lolled back, bouncing with his movements. When he lowered me onto the couch I slow blinked.

"Darling, can you hear me?" My eyes slid shut again. His palm cradled my cheek, fingers dipping into the hair at the nape of my neck.

Darkness overwhelmed me, followed by a blinding, rushing, intense energy blasting into me. It echoed in my chest like a heartbeat. Thump–thump–thump…it pushed out into my limbs, tingling at the very tips of every digit.

I was grabbing onto hair at the back of a head and forcing my tongue into a mouth. Wet and hot and needy, the link between us radiated. *This is familiar.* This great burst of life exploding inside of me, draining out of him. *This is how I killed my foster father.* He came to me in the night and tried to force himself on me, but I took from him instead. *We were both monsters.*

Hands pushed at my shoulders. Issa's tongue entwined with mine even as he fought me. I collapsed back, chest heaving, body tingling. Issa fell onto the coffee table but stood quickly, wobbled slightly, then took two steps away from me. "Holy shit," he said. "I'm sorry." His hair stood out in clumps, his eyes wide, mouth red and swollen.

My heart raced, my breath coming in quick pants. *I can feel everything —every vibrating atom in the whole universe sings the same song, and I can hear it.*

Issa backed away from me, and I moved to the edge of the couch like a string between us pulled me to follow. He raised a hand to his swollen lips, lightly touching them with trembling fingers.

Stand up and take that mouth again! Take every part of him and beg him to take every part of you. But that would kill him…just like it killed my foster father. I balled my hands into fists, nails biting into skin, trying to gain control of myself. "You should go," I said through clenched teeth.

"I..." He paused. "I just never—it's not your fault."

"I need you to go." My voice wavered.

"Please—" He stepped forward.

"Go!" He stumbled back from me. My voice became a force—a wind. "Run!"

He did.

CHAPTER TEN

I DIDN'T HAVE time to dissect what happened with Issa Tor and be on time for band practice. I chose punctuality…*with a side of denial.*

I placed my bow against the strings. Emmanuel caught my eye and smiled at me, all friendly bandmate. I tried to smile back, but fear slipped up my spine and settled into my fingers. *I can't do this.*

Without Megan, I was nothing, and my fingers would prove it with every foible, every slip, every mistake.

I bore down on the violin, holding it tightly, knowing that was wrong but not able to loosen up. *I'm going insane.* Anxiety tightened my grip even more. *Awesomesauce.*

As the band began to play, I waited for my beat and then came in just a moment too early, eager and pathetic. *Scared.*

We did three songs, my performance off every time. Michael began to throw looks at me. *He should be mad. I'm terrible.* I tried harder, my fingers crushing the strings and clutching the bow, wringing out any hint of fluidity.

Michael stopped singing, and Dre's sticks stilled against the drums. Emmanuel's steady bass faded. "Let's take a break," Michael said. He looked over at Emmanuel, jerking his chin at me as if to say, *you deal with her.*

Dre stood and stretched toward the ceiling. Pulling a pack of cigarettes out of his pants pocket, he headed out for a smoke. "I'm going to get some air," Michael said, following him.

I put my bow and fiddle back in their case and looked down at them. "Hey," Emmanuel said behind me. "You need to relax."

"I know." I stared at the glossy wood.

He took my shoulders and turned me around. "I'm going to kiss you now."

"What?" My voice came out strangled.

His hands came to my hips and pulled me flush against the hard planes of his chest. "Is this okay?" he asked, his eyes locked on mine. *It felt way better than just okay.* Zings of lust and need sparkled out of his hands, tingling over my body. My head nodded—my body offering consent while my mind still tripped over itself trying to figure out what was actually happening.

He lowered his mouth to mine, his breath reaching me a moment before his lips covered mine. Energy buzzed between us. It didn't feel dangerous—like I was stealing. It felt good. *Really good.*

Emmanuel's hand wrapped in my hair and moved my head where he wanted it, the sense of power increasing, as if he opened a faucet, letting just the right amount pour through.

My knees weakened and I moaned, my hands fisting in his shirt, pressing hard muscles against my knuckles. The rich scent of honey wafted over me. A melody played in the distance, the song whispering over my skin. *The universe singing again…*

Emmanuel broke the kiss, but I leaned forward, reaching for him. He let me catch him and then bore down on me so that all my senses fuzzed except smell: the strong scent of sweet honey.

I clutched his curls with one hand and let the other wander down his neck, finding the pulse there and laying my fingers over it, moaning softly at the beauty of that beat.

Emmanuel pulled away, bringing his thumb across my lips. "Let's play," he said. I blinked at him. *Play what?* Oh, right. Music.

I uncurled my fingers from his hair, a blush stealing over me. *I can't believe that kiss.*

Emmanuel smiled softly and reached between us to button the top of my blouse. I didn't even realize it had come undone. *That kiss might have melted part of my brain.*

But I didn't feel weak...I felt *alive*.

I heard the door open and turned away, letting my hair fall across my face so that Michael and Dre wouldn't see the bright red flush spreading across my chest, up my cheeks, straight to my hairline. Emmanuel walked over to his bass, his jeans hanging on his hips just so...

He bent over to pick up his instrument, the muscles of his back shifting under the thin material of his T-shirt. *I want to rip it off him.*

What is wrong with me!

I quickly bent down and picked up my violin. It felt different in my hand. The smooth wood, elegant neck, and taut bow *fit* better against me.

Instead of trying to play the song, I melted into it. My eyes closed, and the music washed over me. Michael's voice sang in my blood, the drum pounded in my stomach, and the bass, that low, controlled, never-fading bass, beat in my chest.

CHAPTER ELEVEN

I HELD up a knee-length black dress in front of the mirror. *I look like I'm heading to a funeral.* On stage I liked to wear all black—Megan always fought me on it, insisting that I was hiding away, trying not to be seen. Yeah, she practically had a Ph.D. in Darling psychology.

I miss her. I had no one to talk to about what was happening. I'd gone from a girl who barely tolerated being touched to someone who *needed* to feel skin under me. In the past few days, I'd kissed three men. *Three.*

And two of them didn't give consent that I could remember. *I accosted them.* With Michael I could tell myself we'd been drugged. He even agreed. But with Dr. Tor…what was that about? *Maybe he kissed me?* He was on top. But he had to *force* me away from him.

And then there was Emmanuel. I sat on my bed, clutching the black dress to my chest, wistfully staring out the window but seeing his eyes, feeling his hands, and luxuriating in the memory of *that kiss.*

A shimmer of gold in the closet caught my eye. *Megan's gold shorts.* She'd worn them the night we got our record contract. I pulled them out. That night the music was perfect; we were in sync—as though a force field grew between us, making my fiddle and her voice into one instrument. People said they'd never heard anything like it.

Two months later, days before we were set to begin recording our album, Megan coughed up blood. An expression of abject terror twisted her always-brave face. *She knew what it meant before I did.*

Turning to the mirror, I held the small gold shorts to my waist. They'd fit.

I nodded at my reflection and headed into the bathroom to finish getting ready for the show. I owed it to my bandmates and myself to rock tonight. Megan's little gold shorts were just the thing to help me.

Before leaving the house, I dabbed Gilt onto each of my wrists, behind both ears, and once right between my breasts. "For luck," I said as I replaced the bottle on Megan's dresser. Then with a last look around, I picked up my violin and hit the street.

As I walked over to the venue, I felt eyes on me. Despite the black raincoat I wore, which fell respectably close to my knees, the people I passed dragged their gazes over me. Black stockings and low-heeled black ankle boots, even without seeing the gold shorts, communicated something.

"You look great," Michael said when I walked into the green room. "I like what you did with your hair."

I'd pinned it away from my face, but it flowed in loose, broad curls down my back. "Thanks," I said, nervous about shedding my coat.

Emmanuel sat on a battered couch, his fingers straying over his bass, forearms tensing and relaxing as he watched me cross the room. Turning my back on them, I shrugged out of my coat, exposing the shorts and open back of my shirt. I hung up the coat and turned around.

Both men were staring at me. Michael's jaw hung loose, his eyes fixed on my cleavage. Emmanuel's fingers stilled, his gaze heated. My top was low cut, tight, and black, with the edge of one of Megan's lacy black bras poking over the top.

Michael whistled under his breath, a soft and appreciative sound. "You look incredible."

"Lovely, as always," Emmanuel said, his voice low and rough. He began to strum again, looking down at the instrument.

Are we going back to just being bandmates?

I headed to the refreshment table, picking up a bottle of water and cracking the lid.

It felt like fingers trailed down my spine, and I shivered. Turning, I found Emmanuel's gaze on me—his eyes, usually so warm and calm, were dark and sparkling.

"Can we have a minute?" he asked Michael, without taking his eyes off me.

"Sure, yeah." Michael headed for the door.

Emmanuel stood up slowly, placing his bass gently on the couch. He walked over to the door, his stride lazy. The click of the lock jolted through me.

My heartbeat pulsed through my body. Emmanuel approached slowly, his movements liquid and dead sexy. I bumped up against the table, feeling the edge hit my butt. Putting the bottle of water down behind me, I tried to break from Emmanuel's gaze but couldn't. I literally could not take my eyes off his slow approach.

He stopped inches from me—his breath on my face, his scent swirling around me. Electric vibrations made it feel like we were already touching. I meant to speak, to tell him not to kiss me, but I didn't. *We need to talk, right? That's what people do after they kiss and before they kiss again...*

His hands came up and cupped my face, pulling me up to meet his mouth, and there was nothing in the world but him and me and the spark we made. A tornado of passion unleashed, tearing at me, threatening to destroy us both.

Emmanuel pulled away, his lips still close, and I tried to go after them, but he held me in place, fingers dug deep in my hair, controlling my head. "Stay still." His chest heaved with each breath, and his body shook —like it was taking intense effort to not devour me. *Don't hold back on my account.*

He groaned and closed his eyes, leaning his forehead against mine. "Darling." Emmanuel whispered my name, and it sounded almost like a prayer. *It sounds too damn good.*

I want to tear his shirt off and lick every inch of him.

I surged forward, desperate to take his lips, but he held me back. "No," he whispered. "I won't be able to stop." He sounded pained.

"So don't," I panted, pulling at his shoulders. Leaning up, I captured his lips, wrapping my arms around his neck. His hands dropped to my ass and lifted me onto the table. Pushing between my legs, he took control of the kiss. Water bottles toppled, plastic wrap squeaked, and the table scraped across the floor.

Bright orange and white heat splashed across my closed eyelids. It burned around my body, coursing through my veins at insane speeds. His hand left a trail of flames down my exposed back.

There was knocking at the door. "Yo," Michael's called. "Come on," he yelled when neither of us answered. "It's time to go on!"

Emmanuel did not stop kissing me.

His hand cupped my breast, stroking me through the lacy material. His lips left mine, traveling south. He pulled my hair, tilting my chin skyward. Fingers dipped into the cup of my bra. Emmanuel stilled, staring down at my exposed breast.

Another knock, this one louder. I heard the door handle jiggle, and then Emmanuel's mouth covered my nipple. I cried out, a small, strangled sound that changed into a low moan as he swirled his tongue. "Come on!" Michael yelled. "We don't have time for this."

"I told you I wouldn't be able to stop," Emmanuel said against my breast, the tickle of his lips shooting rays of pleasure and energy to my throbbing center. He returned one hand to my ass, clenching even harder.

"I've got the key," Michael yelled through the door. "I'm coming in, in 3, 2..." Emmanuel turned to look toward the entrance behind him.

"Get out," he growled. Emmanuel's body blocked my view; his hand still on my breast, his neck twisted toward Michael, mere inches from my lips.

"We go on in ten, you asshole."

"I don't give a shit," Emmanuel replied, his voice deep and threatening.

"The fuck you don't give a shit." I heard Michael take several steps into the room.

Emmanuel's hand tensed on my breast. It felt so good. I wanted him so badly.

What the fuck am I doing, spread out on the concession table of a club I'm about to perform in? This isn't professional. This is insane. Holy crap, I've really lost it. The "it" is gone. This has to stop.

I shifted, trying to pull my shirt back up. Emmanuel turned to me, ignoring Michael. "What are you doing?" he asked.

"We're going on."

Both his hands tightened at once, making me ache, desperately hungry for him. His hard length pressed against me. I wanted him so badly it clouded my thoughts, but I wasn't this person. This wanton girl. I pushed him back, yanking my shirt up and closing my legs. He stumbled away, his gaze searing.

"All right," Michael said. "You ready to play? Come on!"

My eyes stayed closed for most of the performance, but I heard the crowd's reaction. *Felt them love every second of it.* Michael's sultry voice, Dre's precision drumming, Emmanuel's bass, and my fiddle made magic.

After it was over, we stumbled off stage, drunk on the music, grinning, knowing we'd done something special. Michael threw an arm around me. "You were incredible," he said.

Our manager, Veronica Haus, a tall woman wearing cowboy boots, tight jeans, a black T-shirt, and a grin, walked into the green room moments after us. "That was amazing!"

"Thanks," Michael answered.

Veronica turned to me. "You were on fire," she said. "I haven't seen you play like that in a year."

I nodded, unable to respond, feeling the joy suck out of the moment. Megan flashed across my vision: her hair disappearing through the door at the hospital, her secret smile just for me. The scent of Gilt rushed up at me. "Thanks," I managed to say.

I can't move on. This is wrong.

Veronica turned back to Michael and grinned at him. I put my violin in its case and then backed toward the door. Emmanuel caught my eye, a warning in his gaze. *We are not done yet.* "Bathroom," I mouthed before slipping out. *I'm a coward.*

I pushed through the crowd and pressed up against the bar. "You were great," Marty, the owner of the club, said.

I smiled and my cheeks warmed. "Thanks."

"No, seriously, Darling. That's one of the best sets I've heard you do. You guys are starting to sound like a band," Marty continued, resting a meaty forearm on the bar and leaning toward me so I could hear him over the din of the crowd. Dread curled in my stomach. If we sounded like a band, then I'd moved on. *But Megan isn't gone!*

"Can you call me a cab?" I asked.

"Leaving so soon?" he frowned. "I thought I saw Thomas Dowerdy from ToneShell Records heading backstage."

"Yeah," I said. "I'm not feeling great."

He nodded, frowning, and stepped toward the phone. A hand tapped my shoulder, and I turned to find Dr. Issa Tor smiling at me. *Ugh. Just what I need to complete this night.* "Hi," he said.

"Hi." I cast my eyes to the bar—a deep, dark wood, thickly lacquered so it shone even in the low light of the club.

"You were great. I didn't realize you played here," Issa continued, acting like I hadn't sexually assaulted him when he tried to bring me soup.

"Only sometimes," I said, playing the game.

"I just moved here, so this is all new to me." He stood close, and as the crowd shifted, he pushed closer. His shoulder brushed against mine. I leaned back into the bar, trying to avoid contact.

"Darling, you still need that cab?" Marty asked, holding up the phone.

"I can drive you home," the doctor offered quickly. "Really, I'd be honored." He leaned into me so that his breath caressed my ear. "I think we should talk. There are things you should know." Marty raised his eyebrows at me. I looked up at Issa; his caramel eyes glowed almost gold as I stared into them.

"What kind of things?"

"Please," Issa said, his gaze darting around. "Not here."

"Okay," I answered, shaking my head at Marty. *Curiosity killed the cat, not the fiddle player.*

"I can carry that for you." Issa reached for my violin.

"No, thanks, I've got it."

He nodded and smiled, looking almost nervous. "My car is right out front." He took my elbow to steer me through the crowd. I pulled free from his touch, afraid of the energy zapping through me.

He respected the distance as we navigated between sweaty bodies, avoiding rocking beers, and making our way out onto the street. A sleek black town car with tinted windows and headlights that looked like glowering eyes waited at the curb.

Issa stepped to the car's back door and opened it for me. The interior overhead lamp went on, lighting black leather seats. There was a driver, I realized. He was wearing a black-brimmed cap, and he didn't turn his head when the door opened.

"Your car?"

"Yes," he answered. "My father is a—" He paused, seeming to search for the right word. "—a diplomat, so I have certain protections."

"Okay," I said, making no move to get into the car.

Issa let go of the door and stepped tentatively toward me. "I promise you that no harm will come to you with me." His voice was smooth and low, the accent slight but decidedly different, like the car and driver. Out of my world.

"What kind of stuff do you think I should know?" I asked.

"Please," he said again, casting a quick glance at the few people smoking by the entrance.

"Give me a hint."

"I know why you always feel so hungry." My eyes narrowed with suspicion. "And I know about your father. Your *real* father." He raised his dark brows at me. *My real father. What the what?* "Please, allow me to drive you home."

Okay...

I climbed into the back seat. The hair that crept from beneath the driver's cap was straight and jet black, like a panther's. In the mirror I saw intense dark eyes, walnut skin, and a bushy mustache. Issa gave him my address.

"Tell me what you know about my father." I kept my hands knotted in my lap, the hunger tickling at my throat, the mention of it like a call, waking it up.

When our eyes met, Issa's went a little hazy. Only my violin case separated our hips. "I'm sorry," he stammered, looking away.

I turned to the window. "For what?" I asked. Out on the busy streets, people smiled, falling against each other—drunk and having fun.

"Darling?" Issa said. My chest clenched, tightening around my heart, squeezing my insides, need spiraling through me. *Emmanuel's lips, his touch —why did I leave?* "Are you okay?" I didn't answer. Issa sighed. "I think we need to talk about what happened the other day. Your...recovery, it's important to me."

I couldn't help but let out a rough laugh. "My recovery," I said, turning to him. "I hardly think what I did was a part of my recovery."

"But that's just it—"

"Sir," the driver spoke without turning around. "The street is blocked."

People streamed across the intersection. They were dressed in shabby clothing, their skin sheet-white, hair gray, patchy, and in disarray. A woman in a hospital gown stumbled by, blood dripping down her arm, a gash on her neck. In her right hand she held a beer.

"It's the zombie run," Issa said. "It must have just finished."

"Right," I said, my voice unsure, fear tingling down my spine.

Issa looked over at me. "I'll walk you to your door." I tried to smile but dread gnawed at me, warring with the desire lining my insides. Issa opened his door, and I clutched my fiddle, taking a deep breath before stepping out into the night.

CHAPTER TWELVE

THE DRIVER, named Basil, followed a couple of paces behind us as we fit ourselves into the stream of runners. Many of them still had numbers on their backs. The block was filled as far as I could see in both directions. Someone brushed up against me, then turned and smiled; his eyes were unfocused, and a line of fake blood traced his neck. "Sorry," he said.

I nodded an acknowledgment of his apology and he continued on, saying something to his friend, who laughed loudly at it. I tried to make myself smaller. Glancing back, it looked like a never-ending stream of people.

"You okay?" Issa asked, drawing my attention. He took my elbow, gently pulling me forward. "Don't worry, I'll get you home safe. And if I fail, Basil is right behind us." He gave me a soft smile. "Nothing gets past Basil."

I looked over my shoulder again. Basil's dark, watchful eyes were trained on us, the sea of people splitting around him. There was something about Basil that people instinctively avoided. A scream rose behind us, and Basil's head whipped around, his hand diving inside his jacket.

The crowd pulsed forward, igniting a chain reaction, and suddenly people ran past me, their arms pumping, dodging those of us who stood still. What started as one scream became a chorus of terror. Basil's arm came around my and Issa's shoulders. He pushed us into a nearby dead end. Buildings rose up on three sides. One of the walls lined with dirty dumpsters, the other windowless with a metal door set into it.

The crowd streamed past. A woman fell, and, letting out a sob, stumbled back to her feet, her head twisted around to watch the approaching danger behind her. Ignoring her bloodied knees, the fresh, real stuff looking bright and lurid compared to the dried, fake gore that clung to her neck and shoulder, she began to run again.

Issa stepped up next to Basil at the edge of the alley. "Sir, we need to get you out of here." A shot rang out, followed by three more, and then an anguished yelp. I backed up until I hit the far wall, clutching my violin case to my chest like a shield...like a lover.

"We should run for it," Issa said. His eyes were wide, and a lock of dark hair curling over his forehead bounced as he looked from me back to the street, and then to me again. He held his hand out and I stared at it, keeping mine clutched around my instrument.

Shots fired again, closer this time, and Issa turned, clearing my view to the street. Basil stood over two men, his gun aimed at a hunched figure ravaging another on the ground. The legs of the victim shook against the pavement. The attacker did not flinch as Basil fired, hitting him in the back. Basil shifted his aim to the attacker's head and—pow!— the figure collapsed over its victim, the body spasming beneath its slumped form.

Basil took one step, positioned his gun over the head of the victim on the ground and fired. I tasted blood in my mouth. I'd bitten my lip. Basil looked up, toward where the screaming started, and dropped the clip from his gun; it bounced once when it hit the pavement. He turned toward Issa as he pulled a spare clip from inside his coat. "Sir, you need to go now." He jammed the clip into place and raised his gun.

Issa took my arm and pulled me forward. I stumbled at first, but as we came out of the alley, I looked where Basil was pointing his gun and adrenaline released into my system, shocking me into action. Figures stumbled forward—just like that woman at the parade. *This isn't a drug...*

With Issa's strong hand on my arm I pounded forward, running faster than I ever had, dodging abandoned belongings as we flew toward my apartment. *Just around the corner and we'll be there.*

Gunshots sounded behind us, and I took just the sparest second to turn my head before dodging left, down my block, Issa with me. In that brief glance I saw chaos and smoke, some still, slumped figures, and others spasming in seizure.

I skidded to a stop ten paces from my apartment entrance. There was a body blocking my door, face a bloody pulp except for the terrifying specter of white teeth where the mouth ought to be, shaking uncontrollably.

People streamed by me, screaming, and crying. Issa bent down to examine the jogger. "Don't," I warned.

The body on the ground lunged for Issa, those white teeth open and the stump of a tongue straining toward his neck. Issa threw himself away from the creature, who grabbed his ankle, pulling it toward what remained of its mouth. Raising my violin case above my head, I slammed it down onto the thing's wrist, but it didn't release Issa's ankle. The case blocked its mouth, though—the creature gnawing at the rough black exterior.

Blood oozed from horrific wounds. Its glassy eyes shifted, noticing my ankle. It tensed to lunge, but the back of its head blew off. "Where is your apartment?" Basil asked. Blood was splattered all over his crisp white shirt and dark suit jacket.

"There," I said using my chin to point at the door next to him.

He looked at it. "Key?"

I reached into the pocket of my raincoat. Basil raised his gun, pointing it at me. "Duck," he said.

I dropped to the ground, crouching next to my violin case, pulling it close. Basil fired, and a body crumpled behind me, its limbs loud against the pavement with no attempt to break its fall.

Another shot rang out and the same thud. "Sir, get the keys," I heard Basil say as he fired again, and again.

Issa pulled me up and took the keys from my hand. He hustled me over to the door. I held my violin case flush to my chest, my back against the wall, as Issa put the key into the lock.

A man with gray hair and a giant bite out of his neck that exposed tendons and torn-open veins grabbed Issa. Blood poured in long, thick lines down his chest. Teeth bared, he pulled on Issa's arm, knocking the keys to the ground.

Issa grabbed the man's shoulders, keeping the chomping teeth at bay. His back slammed against the wall next to me, the muscles in his forearms standing out in strong bands. I stuck my violin case between the teeth of the zombie and Issa's face.

Issa's arms gave out, and the creature slumped against the case, pinning Issa to the wall. Then Basil was behind the zombie, stabbing it at the base of the skull, angling up.

It slumped, like a wind-up toy that's suddenly run out of turns, and when Basil withdrew his knife, pushing against the dead man's shoulder for leverage, the body fell to its knees and then to the side, its face landing at my feet. A hand grabbed my shoulder, and I swung my violin case, screaming, my whole body repulsed at the touch.

What was once a woman stumbled away from me and, seeing Issa still leaning against the wall, launched herself at him so hard that his head knocked against the brick, bounced, and flopped onto his chest. Basil was instantly on the zombie, wrapping his arm around its neck, pulling it back from Issa, driving the knife through the thing's temple, as Issa slid to the ground, unconscious.

Fighting through my terror, I scrambled across the pavement to where my keys sparkled from a crack in the cement. My fingers closed around them and a sudden weight pushed me—I stumbled forward, landing on my knees, the weight following me, pushing me onto my hands.

I threw an elbow, knocking the thing off my back and then twisting myself around so I could at least face my death. A zombie with long hair, still half in a ponytail, launched at me, its speed and hunger far greater than mine. *This is the end.*

Her hands—still hot, still human—gripped my shoulders, and her wide-open mouth came at my face. I tried to get my hands up, to stop her somehow, but suddenly she flew off me in an elegant arc. Her body landed in the middle of the street, splatting in front of a fleeing runner, who screamed, leaped over it, and kept going.

A figure stood above me, and I swiped at my eyes, trying to clear them. *Impossible.* "Megan?"

"Yes, Darling," she said. "It's me."

CHAPTER THIRTEEN

MEGAN STOOD OVER ME, her bright red hair even more brilliant than before she got sick. The colors were vibrant and varied—every shade from burgundy to gold represented in her long, wavy locks. *Impossible.*

White, smooth skin, touched with bright pink at her lips and cheeks, defied reality. She looked like a doll made from the finest porcelain. Too beautiful to be real.

"Did any blood get in your mouth?" she asked.

I just stared up at her. She crouched down, moving so fast that her hair floated around her for a moment while gravity caught up. *Impossible.*

"Did it get in your mouth?" she asked again, her voice low and earnest. I reached a hand out to touch her face, but she wrapped her fingers around mine before I could reach her cheek. Megan's skin was cold. *Deathly cold.* A shiver traveled down my wrist and along my arm.

Megan leaned closer to me, her eyes scanning my mouth. She sniffed, as if smelling me. *What in the what?* Then smiled, her shoulders relaxing. "You bit your lip," she said.

"We have to go," a man behind her said. Megan turned to him, but I just stared at her, looking at the elegant length of her neck, the veins almost violet under her pale skin. *Megan is alive. How is this…what in the…*

"I know," Megan answered the man, her tone peevish. She turned back to me. "Can you stand?" she asked.

The man came around Megan and crouched down next to me. Megan put her hand on his shoulder. "She does not like to be touched, Dimitri."

"It won't be a problem," he assured her, reaching toward me.

I tore my attention off Megan to look at him. Dimitri's eyes were the pale blue of thick ice and the edges of a hot flame. His cheekbones sculpted from marble, lips red as a rose petal and turned up into a predatory smile. I recognized him... but from where?

My brain felt fuzzy—as if I was thinking through a veil.

"She will walk." Megan said it like a warning. Dimitri frowned, his lips turning almost pouty—except those lips could never be anything but cruel...could they?

He shrugged, and stood, relenting to Megan. *I've seen him before.*

His tailored suit, charcoal gray with burgundy and black thread running through it, moved with him...like a second skin. *I know him. What is wrong with my mind right now? Why can't I place this guy?*

He straightened his tie—narrow and matte black—before crossing behind Megan over to where a zombie pinned Basil against my apartment building wall. Dimitri walked like a dancer—movements liquid, precise, controlled and strong. *I bet he can dance the tango and leap like a ballerino.*

Grabbing the creature around its neck, Dimitri's fingers tightened, pressing through the flesh. The head popped off, flying sideways and bouncing on the ground. The rest of the body crumpled at his feet. Dimitri shook his hand and bits of flesh flew off it. *That is disgusting, why don't I care? I must be in shock. Did I hit my head?*

Basil straightened his jacket and thanked Dimitri, who gave a small shake of his head as if to say it was nothing, then removed a handkerchief from his inside pocket and wiped at his hands. He turned, his gaze finding mine and he winked. *Winked!*

Something in my brain clicked. He was *The Stranger*—in the hospital, at the parade before the attack, and outside my apartment...he frightened the cat. *He frightens me.* And more...

"What is going on?" I asked.

"Don't worry," Megan said, and the veil over my mind seeming to thicken into a blanket, so that my memories of Dimitri became shadows at the corner of my mind.

My gaze landed on Issa's unconscious body. "We can't leave them," I said, my tongue thick. *I sound drunk.*

Megan took the keys from me and unlocked the front door. I sat on the pavement and watched, Dimitri standing over me, his presence seeming to keep the chaos at bay. Not only did the zombies avoid us, but my thoughts themselves eased at his presence. *I don't mind if he carries me. No, not at all.*

"4G," Megan told Basil, holding the door wide. He didn't waste time. Grabbing Issa by the arm, he slung the taller man over his shoulder, and, taking the offered keys, disappeared inside. Megan closed it behind them and gestured toward a navy blue SUV idling at the curb. "We need to go."

"My violin." The case lay on the ground by the wall. It was scuffed up, smears of blood on its rough black exterior, but still intact. Megan picked it up in a blur of movement. She took my hand and pulled me to my feet. *I need to speak with Issa, don't I? Isn't there something I was doing?* "He was going to tell me—"

Megan cut me off. "We have to go now." Sirens wailed in the distance and screaming still filled the air, but I felt no fear. Megan opened the back door and helped me in. A zombie fell against the opposite window, its palms pressed flat to the glass, viscous, blood-laced drool seeping from its mouth. Megan closed my door. The creature flew backward, and Megan was sitting next to me by the time it hit the building across the street.

"I need to blindfold you," she said.

"What?" I asked.

"Just trust me."

"Trust you," I parroted.

"Yes," she nodded.

"Okay." *I always trust Megan.*

She smiled, relieved. Dimitri, sitting in the driver's seat, passed her a black hood. Megan pulled it over my head, engulfing me in darkness.

The sirens were closer now, loud over the sound of our engine as we started forward. The rat-tat-tat of gunfire made me jump. Megan wrapped her hand around mine, and the fog in my mind thickened.

I can't believe she is really here. The longer we drove, the less I believed it. The sirens faded, our speed increased, and soon I heard nothing but the engine, my breathing, and the whine of our tires over blacktop.

Without the sight of her and only experiencing Megan's smooth, cold, hard fingers interlaced with mine, I began to feel as though I was holding hands with a statue rather than a person. *It is impossible that Megan is a person.* Her body *should* be weak and riddled with disease. She *should* be dead.

Instead, she exhibited speed and strength beyond the bounds of biology.

My world, which had always felt disjointed and confused but anchored by Megan, now seemed completely untethered.

People with fatal wounds, still fresh and lurid, were rising up and stumbling through the streets, looking for their own victim.

Megan was dying. Megan disappeared. Megan was here, with me.

I climbed into the kitchen cabinet of a two-room cabin my father built and was discovered by police in a completely different place.

Gravel crunched under the tires, and we rolled to a slow stop. The driver's door opened and closed. "Darling," Megan said. *Her voice saying my name sounds so right.* "I will take the hood off once we get you inside."

My door opened. The air was cooler here, fresher. Megan's voice in front of me now. "Come on." She took my hand. A gentle touch held the back of my head down as I climbed out. *Like I am a prisoner getting out of a cop car.*

"I'll carry her; it's better," Dimitri said. His voice was smooth, the hint of an accent I couldn't place. "I promise you she will not mind," he assured Megan. *He's right.*

"No," Megan said, her voice low and stern. She led me, holding my hand over gravel, then grass. A gentle breeze rustled leaves. The tinkling sound of a stream mixed with the vibration of crickets. "There are stairs coming up," Megan said. "Here they are. Raise your foot." I did as I was told, and we traveled up four steps. They did not creak or wheeze like wood. The smoothness of them made me think I was walking on stone. This sensation continued as we moved indoors.

The air warmed, and I could smell the lingering scent of smoke from a wood fire. Our footsteps echoed, so I guessed the room was large. "I'm taking off the hood now," Megan said quietly, her breath moving against the fabric. She lifted it, and I blinked for a moment while my eyes focused. That's when I realized hers had changed. While one eye was still the moss green I remembered, the other was frosty blue, just like Dimitri's. "You're okay, Darling," she said. "Everything is okay."

I felt my lips moving with hers, and my mind agreeing. She smiled and then stepped to my side, her arm sliding through mine. It was an achingly familiar gesture. The sweet intimacy of our sides touching was something I'd relished. But Megan's body felt harder now, not the soft flesh I'd once known. This person next to me wasn't Megan…*my friend is dead but not gone.*

CHAPTER FOURTEEN

I'D BEEN RIGHT that the room was large. A former bank, maybe. A crystal chandelier hung from the domed ceiling, several of its bulbs burned out and a thick layer of dust dulling its sparkle. There was a mezzanine; its banister carved white marble. Oriental carpets covered the floor, worn leather couches and chairs faced each other. A grand fireplace, its white surface stained black, was the centerpiece of the seating area.

"You're back, Megan," a woman said as she entered the room through a door to the left of the fireplace. "And you've brought your friend." She clapped her hands together. "Wonderful."

The woman's hair, parted in the center, fell straight to her waist in a sheet of shimmering gold. Black pants clung to her thin hips and long legs. A loose red blouse made of satin seemed to float around her as she crossed the room toward us.

She had the same skin as Megan: smooth, flawless cream with dashes of pink on the lips and cheekbones. Her eyes were that same strange blue as Dimitri.

"Darling," Megan said. "I want you to meet my mother, Pearl Quick."

What the what? Megan's parents are long dead...

"I've wanted to meet you for so long." She smiled at me, her teeth straight and white. "Call me Pearl."

She clasped my hand in both of hers. The coldness of her skin raised goose bumps across my forearms. She looked young, not much older than Megan, if not the same age. *Impossible. This is all impossible.*

"Please, let's sit down." Pearl waved one of her arms toward the couch. The elegant gesture stole my breath—the invitation felt impossible to refuse.

"Grab us some drinks?" she asked Dimitri, then looked over at Megan. "You must be thirsty, dear."

"No," Megan said, following us over to the couches.

"Dimitri, bring Darling some water and"—she narrowed her eyes, searching my face— "some brandy. I know you've had quite a shock. And bring something for Megan and me; we must keep our strength up during these difficult times."

"No," Megan said again. Her mother's face darkened as she turned to her. Megan seemed to shy away from the other women's stare. "Sorry," Megan said.

Dimitri left the room, his hard-soled shoes loud in the tall space.

Pearl sat on one of the couches and pulled me down next to her. Megan took a seat in a high-backed leather chair facing us. Pearl opened a small lacquered box on the coffee table and took out a filterless cigarette.

She lit it and settled herself against the cushions, sticking out her tongue and plucking a piece of tobacco off it. Pearl smiled, gesturing with the cigarette. "A habit left over from my human days."

"Human days?" My brain tried to understand, but it just kept clicking over, nothing becoming clearer, that damn haze smothering me.

"Yes, Darling. We are not human. And neither are those things that attacked you."

I looked over at Megan. She sat on the edge of her seat, elbows on her knees, hands clasped. She nodded.

"You're not alive?" I asked.

Megan frowned, her brows furrowing. "Not in the way that you are."

"But she is not entirely like me either," Pearl said.

The door opened and Dimitri returned, holding a silver tray. He lowered it in front of Pearl, and she handed two crystal glasses to me, one filled with water, the other brandy. I took them but did not move to drink.

I'm not thirsty...I feel almost nothing. "Drink," Pearl said. "The water first, like it's medicine, and then you can sip the brandy."

I did as she directed, gulping down the water so fast some dribbled off my chin as I finished. Pearl took the glass back and placed it on the tray.

Megan and Pearl's cups brimmed with red, thick liquid. "It's blood," Pearl answered my unasked question. She took a sip, and when she lowered the glass, her top lip was stained. The tip of her tongue came out and licked it clean. "We live off blood."

"You're vampires?" I asked. I felt no fear.

She shrugged. "We are the basis of that myth."

"And those things we saw?" I asked.

"Zombies," Megan answered.

"Have some brandy," Pearl said, and I took a small sip. "Megan, drink."

I looked over at Megan. Dark circles had appeared under her eyes as she stared into the cut crystal glass in her hand. She shook her head, lips tightening into a firm line of defiance. *She looks almost human again, like the young determined woman I know...and love.*

"Drink," Pearl commanded, her voice hard. Megan's hand shook as it approached her lips. "Now," Pearl hissed. Megan's lips curled back and her incisors grew, reaching toward the blood that approached. The hunger in her eyes didn't look human at all. A spark of emotion penetrated the veil, and Pearl's head whipped to me, her eyes soothing the feelings away.

"Megan is still new." Pearl smiled at me, all friendly new acquaintance. "She cannot control her fangs."

Megan gave in, the glass clasped to her lips, tipping up in a blur of motion, and then it was on the coffee table, empty. Megan swiped at her mouth and sat back, staring at her mother, resentment oozing off of her.

"Sip your brandy, Darling," Pearl said to me, her voice light. Sweet and sharp, it burned all the way down. "Now." Pearl placed her hand on my thigh. "I'm going to explain some things to you. I will continue to use my influence so that you remain calm, but this will be hard."

"Your influence?"

Pearl nodded. "You feel it already." Ah, *the gauzy sensation. They are doing this to me.* "Part of our transformation is more control over our own emotions. With time we also learn to control others."

I nodded, calm, and at ease.

"Good." Pearl smiled. *She is so lovely.* "You have my daughter's blood, and that is why I've brought you here."

"You left her," I said. "You abandoned her when she was just a child. Do you know what happened to her?" A million times I'd thought about Megan's parents—*druggies who never gave a shit,* is how Megan put it. I'd spent so much of my life hating them, wondering what kind of monsters could leave someone as special as Megan. The weight of Pearl's influence allowed me to feel dispassionate about a topic that had always felt like a wound.

Pearl raised an eyebrow. "Her father and I were turned when she was very young. We could not take her with us."

"That's bullshit," I said without anger; it felt like a fact, simple and true. "You were on drugs. She was in and out of the system until you finally disappeared. Do you know what happened to her? To us? Did you know when it was happening?"

Pearl frowned. "Darling, this is not the time for that discussion. The world as you know it is coming to an end."

"That already happened," I said, "when Megan disappeared."

Pearl shook her head, a small line of frustration forming between her brows. "No, Darling, I mean that all of humanity is in danger. We believe that the scales have tipped and your species has finally done it. We brought you here today to save you."

"Save me how?"

"To turn you."

"Turn me?"

Megan spoke then. "Darling, you need to become like us or you'll die...or worse."

"Worse?"

Pearl nodded. "You'll either be turned by us, a zombie or—"

"Or become a blood bag," a man's deep rumble finished Pearl's sentence. I twisted to see a devastatingly handsome man crossing the room toward us. *He must have come down the stairs.*

His jet black hair was slicked back from his face, exposing a strong nose, chiseled jaw, and those same light, penetrating blue eyes. "Not that you would mind." He smiled that same predatory smile Dimitri did.

Megan stood in a flash.

He laughed, the sound bouncing off the walls. "Don't worry," he said. "I'm not going to drink from her. But someone should explain the other option."

Megan growled. "No one is going to touch her."

The man smiled at me. "Megan, don't you want to introduce me to your friend?"

"This is my father, Brad." He extended his hand, standing above me, his eyes glittering. I took it. Brad's skin, like his wife and daughter's, was smooth and cold. *Not alive.*

Megan sat down next to me, and her father moved away. "You have a decision to make," Megan said, her voice low and tight.

"How can I make a decision if I'm being influenced?"

Megan looked over at her mother. "Give her a little room, Mom." Pearl lifted her hand from my thigh and panic rose. "Not that much," she said. The blanket of comfort wrapped around my shoulders again. Megan smiled at me. "Simply put, the zombies are rising. It is prophesied that they will take over the world. We need to protect humans."

"Prophesied by who?"

Brad sat down in the leather chair across from us and laced his fingers together, elbows resting on the chair's arms. "It is written in our religious texts."

"That's it?" I asked. He raised his eyebrows. I shrugged. "There are so many religions and beliefs, how can you know that yours is right?"

"Faith," he answered.

"Is it your faith that drives you to protect humans, or is it because we are your food?"

Pearl huffed out a laugh. "I like her. She's funny when she isn't scared."

"Food is a simplification," Megan said, ignoring her mother. "The fact is, Darling, zombies are spreading—we can't stop it."

Megan's father picked up Pearl's glass of blood. Taking a sip, his lips twisted. "I don't know how you drink it like that."

Megan took my hand in hers. "Listen to me, Darling. You have to become one of us, or you'll be forced into camps."

"Camps?"

Pearl answered. "We've been preparing. You may not believe in our prophecy, but it is coming true. In order to survive, we've built compounds all around the world to keep humans safe."

"The cost of entry," Megan's father said with a smile, "is a small blood donation."

I nodded understanding. "You need us to survive, so you'll keep us alive. At least enough to keep you going." *It didn't bother me. Just a fact. As cold and real as their skin.*

Her father smiled. "She gets it."

"So, you see, Darling," Megan said, "you need to become one of us so that you don't have to..."

"Become a blood bag," her father said again with a smile. "But, what Megan is leaving out, is that it feels *really good*." He rolled the words "really" and "good" around with his tongue, turning them dirty.

"No," Megan said. "Not her."

"You know how pleasurable it is," Pearl admonished. "She should be given the option."

"No," Megan said again.

Dimitri spoke then; I'd forgotten all about him. He stood like a statue next to the fireplace. "I'll do it," he said.

"Good," Megan's father stood. "That's perfect."

Megan's hand tightened on mine to the point of pain. I felt it through the haze of the influence, and I grabbed onto it, using the pain as a line back to myself, out from under the cape they'd thrown over me. "No," Megan said. "I'll do it."

Pearl shook her head. "You know you can't."

"Why?" I asked.

Pearl turned to me. "You are of the same blood. We do not feed off our own blood."

"Same blood?"

"Our blood pact," Megan said with a small smile. "We promised."

"That's why we are taking time out from this war to bring you in," Pearl said.

All the vampires in the room cocked their heads at once. "We must go," Megan's father said, suddenly standing. "Dimitri, take her to her room."

"Can't –" Megan began, but her father glared at her.

"You will come with us," he said, his voice that same commanding tone Pearl had used earlier. Megan went to speak. "Not another word." He cut her off—and a wave of something crossed the room. Megan stood, as did her mother, and then they were gone in a blur. The front door slammed behind them, and I was alone with Dimitri.

Without their influence panic crashed. My throat closed, and tears filled my eyes; that deep and terrifying hunger in my gut began to grow outward, taking over my limbs.

Images battered my brain. My dad in the woods. Megan's blue eye. Her father's menacing smile. The blood staining the tip of Pearl's tongue. The open mouth of a starving zombie…

CHAPTER FIFTEEN

My hand holding the brandy shook, the golden liquid sloshing. Dimitri strolled over and stood looking down at me as I hyperventilated.

He sat next to me and put his hand over mine, taking the glass then placing his fingers against my wrist. Warmth spread throughout my body, weighing a thick layer of calm over me.

"There now," he said with a smile. "Come with me, I'll show you to your room."

"I have a room?"

"Yes, we expect you to stay."

"But how can I decide what to do with all of you controlling me?"

He smiled. "Maybe we will make the decision for you."

"But Megan—"

"She's not in charge."

"Who is? Not you. You get the drinks."

He chuckled. "A man like me is not meant to lead."

"Why not?"

"You ask a lot of questions."

I realized he was holding my hand, and we were strolling down a hallway. *How did that happen?* The carpet was red with a gold paisley pattern. Dusty oil paintings decorated the walls, which were once white but now stained yellow with age. "This is your room." Dimitri stopped at an open door.

A canopy bed with curtains the same powdery violet as dawn took up the center of the room. Beyond it, a sitting area with a love seat and coffee table fit into a bay window. Drapes the color of golden hay closed out the night. A dressing table with a round mirror and a cushioned stool completed the "Princess in a Tower" motif.

Dimitri released me, but I still felt his warmth. "Why are you warm?" I asked.

"Because you like it."

"How do you know?"

"I can feel you."

"Can every vampire feel me like that?"

"No, the older you get the more..." he paused. "Don't think about that now, Darling. Come." He walked me over to the bed.

Sitting down he placed me in front of him so that our faces were at the same level. "Were you following me?" I asked.

His lips curled up, and his eyes darkened. "Yes. It was very enjoyable."

"Why? Are you going to turn me? Were you hunting me?" A small zing of emotion shot up from my stomach. *Fear or lust?* I couldn't tell.

Dimitri laughed softly. "Not hunting, no. Watching." The way he said it made it sound even more dangerous than being hunted. *What does he want from me? What would I refuse him?* "I won't turn you now," he assured me.

"Who are you?"

"My name is Dimitri."

I shook my head, frustration pulling at the gauze. "I know that. Where are you from?"

"Originally?" He took a breath. *Scenting me?* "It no longer matters."

"How old are you?" His eyes glimmered with amusement. Desire edged out frustration and began to tease the gauze apart. *I want to touch his face, to see his fangs. He is so beautiful.*

Hunger broke through a patch of his control...or was he making me feel this way?

"Much older than you," he answered.

"Older than Pearl?"

He nodded. "Yes, about eight centuries older."

Dimitri measures his life in centuries...

My palm touched his cheek—smooth like porcelain, but not cold. *He feels alive.* Confusion clouded his gaze. *He's been confused by me before...*the first time I saw him in the hospital. Dimitri's hand grabbed my wrist.

"What is happening?" I asked, as the heat between us grew, my arm burning where he held me. I reached out with my other hand but he shied away, grabbing my wrist and stopping me. I leaned in, drawn to his mouth, the color alluring, the cruel twitch of his smile enthralling.

When our lips touched, it stung, and I snapped back...though not far. His pupils grew, turning his pale blue eyes almost black. I reached for him again, and this time his lips met mine, and I breathed in searing heat.

He opened his mouth and, releasing my wrists, brought his hands to cup my face. I tentatively licked a fang and he growled. The taste of blood bloomed.

He groaned, and energy coursed through me. Dimitri twisted, taking me with him, slamming my body onto the bed, his lips never leaving mine.

My fingers dug into his hair—hunger riding me. *I can't kill him.* I could unleash upon him and he could take it.

"What are—" Dimitri didn't get to finish his thought.

He was gone in a blur of motion. Suddenly, I was just looking up at the canopy above me, my fingers holding nothing but air.

I pushed up onto my elbows. Dimitri held Megan by her throat, her feet six inches above the carpet. She didn't look like she was struggling to breathe. Which made sense—why would a vampire need to breathe?

"What are you doing? Let her go," I said.

Dimitri looked at me, his eyes huge and black—fathomless. *I can step into them and disappear.* His lips were parted, fangs exposed. A shiver of desire raced over my skin. He was at once terrifying and beautiful. *I want him.* "Let her go." Energy coursed through me.

Dimitri's eyes narrowed. "I will taste you again." He dropped Megan and stalked toward me.

"She is mine," Megan said, her voice rough.

His head whipped to her. "You cannot claim your own blood."

"I just did," Megan answered, stepping close to him, so that their chests touched. Her fangs slowly grew as she looked up at him. *My best friend has fangs.*

Dimitri's hands fisted at his side. "You are a fool. I will speak to your father."

"I've already talked to him." Megan jutted her chin up. "Now go."

Dimitri looked over at me again, his eyes trailing down to my shirt. I followed his gaze and found it ripped, my bra exposed. *When did that happen?*

"Do you agree to this?" he asked, his voice low and seductive. "Will you allow her to claim you?"

"I have a choice?" I asked, an inkling of surprise bubbling up from under the layer of suppression they'd thrown over me.

"No," Megan said. "You don't. Get out, Dimitri."

He growled, the sound vibrating through the room, shaking the drapery on the bed. *He does not sound human.*

Then he was gone—the door left open in his wake.

Megan crossed to the bed. "Are you okay?" she asked, touching the ripped edge of my shirt.

I looked down at myself—the black lace bra, gold shorts, and stockings. "Yes," I said. "I was enjoying that, actually."

"I couldn't let him feed on you."

"Why not? What does it mean that I am yours?" I looked into her mismatched eyes, concentrating on the familiar one, avoiding the hungry gaze of the icy fiery blue orb.

"Now I'm the only one who can feed off you. But don't worry, I'm not going to. You're safe."

"What will you eat?"

"Don't worry about me, Darling." Megan smiled, and for a moment, she looked so much like herself—fearless and commanding. Just like before she fell ill.

"I got used to worrying about you," I said.

Megan nodded, her lips tightening. "You don't need to anymore. I'll take care of you again." She went to a dresser and pulled out a big sleeping shirt. "Here." She held it out to me.

I changed into it and got under the covers, resting my head on the soft pillow. Megan laid down on top of the covers next to me.

She curled up on her side, and we looked into each other's eyes, like we always had when we were scared, when either of us needed comfort. "How did you get your parents to let you claim me?" I asked.

"We struck a deal." She broke eye contact, rolling onto her back and looking up at the canopy.

"Can they control you?"

"Sort of," she answered.

"Do you sleep?" I asked.

"No, but I can lie still with you."

Megan was still, I noticed then. It was something else that had changed about her. The wildness that had always surrounded her, the frenetic energy that seemed to come from within, was gone. There was an unnatural stillness about her now. *Right, because she isn't breathing.*

"I'm relieved," I said

"Because I'm alive?" Megan asked, looking over at me.

"Are you?"

She turned her gaze back to the canopy. "Sort of."

"I'm glad to see you, but I'm also afraid of you. You're not the same."

"No, I'm not." Megan glanced my way. "But I still love you, Darling. I think I love you even more."

"I love you, too." *And I always will.*

She smiled and reached out, pushing a strand of hair off my face. "I missed you." Her cool fingers grazed my cheek. Tears welled in my eyes, but Megan cooled the emotions. "No need for that," she said in a soft whisper.

Sleep pressed at me. "I don't think I'm crazy." My voice was thick with exhaustion. "That's why I'm relieved. I think my memories of my father are real. It makes sense now."

"How?" Megan asked, turning her body toward mine again, her eyebrows conferencing, the weight of her will lessening, allowing me to answer.

"I don't know. Why do you drink blood? Why are your parent's vampires? Why are zombies overrunning the streets?" I paused. "Then again, maybe I am crazy, and none of this is real."

"It's real, Darling," Megan said, closing her eyes. "It is written."

"What is?"

"The rise of the zombies, the fall of the human race," she answered.

"By who?"

"God," she said, opening her eyes. They glittered in the dull light of the bedroom.

"Since when do you believe in God?" I asked, my voice barley a whisper.

"I was supposed to die. Instead, I'm stuck in some kind of limbo. My parents—who never attended church, and I thought were long dead—are vampires. Religious vampires. I don't think believing in a higher power is such a leap."

"Does it hurt?"

"What?"

"Being in limbo?"

"Only if I don't drink blood."

"Does it taste good?"

She nodded. "Delicious." Her fangs descended a little. She rolled away from me, looking back up at the canopy. *Hiding from me.*

"Does it feel good to be fed on? Like your father said?"

"Yes," she sighed. "When we take it from a human directly, it feels very good for everyone involved."

"But you don't kill people."

"It's not necessary."

"But...?" I said, sensing she had more to say.

"It feels the best." She licked her lips. "Let's not talk about this. Go to sleep, Darling."

"Okay," I said, my eyelids heavy again. I let them close and began slipping into a deep sleep. I tried to resist it for a moment.

"Shhh," Megan said, her cool fingers on my cheek again. "Sleep."

And I did. There were no dreams, no restlessness...nothing but slumber.

CHAPTER SIXTEEN

WHEN I WOKE, my limbs felt heavy. I didn't open my eyes right away, just sank into the lethargy. As my awareness broadened, disorientation set in. *Where am I?*

Wriggling my toes against soft sheets, I blinked my eyes open and saw violet curtains... understanding blossomed. The whole truth of it vibrated in my cells. *The world has gone mad.* Making me normal.

I climbed out of the bed, and my legs almost buckled under me. Using the mattress for support, I stumbled toward the mirror. Sitting on the cushioned stool, I met my own gaze—emerald green eyes sparkled back at me. *A precious stone struck by the sun.* My midnight black hair was tangled, as if I'd slept a week rather than a night. My lips looked kissed, plump and rosy. The big T-shirt I wore slipped off one shoulder. *I look beautiful...and sexy.*

Blinking, I stared at myself, as surprised by that simple thought as anything else happening... I'd never seen myself like this before—as a person worth wanting.

I tried to sense if I was under another being's control. *Yes.* I felt a bind on me, like a tourniquet cutting off blood supply. A sense that there was more of me, but I couldn't reach it. This was different than the gauze— not as opaque. It almost felt like this was something I could snap... releasing my full self.

Using the makeup table for support, I reached out toward the bed. My vision darkened at the edges, and I paused, regaining my balance. There was a robe on the couch. A silver carafe and white china cup sat on the low table. Steadier, I crossed the room, picking up the robe and shrugged into it. It was thin cotton, pure white, with a thick black tie.

I headed for the door, wanting to find Megan, ready to leave this place. I needed to go home, shower, and think about all this without their influence. *Untie this tourniquet.*

The door was locked. A small wave of fear passed through me, raising goose bumps across my flesh, but it faded, leaving me calm and thirsty.

Returning to the small couch, I picked up the silver carafe. Popping open the lid, I confirmed it was coffee before pouring myself a cup. No milk or sugar was provided, so I drank it black, waiting in the big room, my mind an almost pleasant blank…the calm before the storm.

The clinkety-clank of a key drew my attention to the door. Megan walked in, wearing tight jeans and a black T-shirt, carrying a plate piled high with pastries. "I brought you some breakfast." She closed the door behind her.

"Am I a prisoner?" I asked as she crossed the room.

"No, of course not."

"Then why is my door locked?" My voice sounded strange—almost echoey.

Megan put the plate on the coffee table. "I just didn't want you wandering around while I was gone." She sat down next to me. "Or anyone coming in here without my permission."

"You say that so casually." Megan didn't respond. My thoughts were stuck in a kaleidoscope, colorful and fragmented, parts of a whole I could not make out. "Can I go home?" I asked.

"It's too dangerous," she said.

"What if you came with me?" *That would be wonderful. For us to just go home together.*

Megan shook her head. "I can't, Darling." She reached out and took my hand. "I really think you should change," she sighed. "Become a vampire. You'll be safe." Her voice dropped an octave. "We could be together."

I stared at her hand in mine—the sensation that I was touching a statue returning. *I don't want to be like that.* But I wanted to be with Megan. "What is it like to be fed on?"

She turned away from me, releasing my hand. "No one ever fed on me."

I swallowed, my thoughts moving slowly. "Okay, then what does it feel like to feed...on a person?"

She licked her lips, and a wave of hunger pulsed off of her. "It's the best feeling I've ever felt." Megan didn't look at me.

"I want to be with you, Megan. You know I do...but I don't know if I can..." Her eyes slowly met mine, one that green I remember so well, the other fiery blue—*starving.* "Can you feed on me?"

"It's not safe." She stood in a blur and paced away from me.

"Why?" Her eyes met mine, the pupils large and black. All I'd ever wanted was to give Megan everything she needed. "The closer to death I take a human, the better it feels," she said, her fangs descending. *I want to feed her.*

"Have you?" I swallowed, fear trickling through the tourniquet. "Killed?"

She didn't answer right away, instead staring at her feet for a long moment. Finally she nodded. Megan *killed* someone. "I didn't understand," she said. "At first I didn't know how to stop. I have more control now." She brought her eyes to meet mine, the pupils larger, as if the memory of that death made her even hungrier. "It's against our religion to drink the last drop."

"That's good, I guess." Human life seemed so inconsequential while under their control.

"The act of feeding is sacred to my family."

"Feed on me." The words came out almost unbidden. *Did I mean that?* Yes. We could be together...

"I want to." Her fangs fully descended, pushing into her lower lip.

I pulled my hair aside, exposing my neck in invitation. Megan's gaze riveted to my throat. My pulse pounded against my skin, as if the blood *wanted* her to drink it.

She moved in a blur—covering me with her body. Sharp pain melted into delicious sensation. Her hands held my back, pressing my body tight to her.

It was the most perfect our relationship had ever been: I was nourishing her. She was taking the excess in me and turning it into fuel. Into life. *This is meant to be between us.*

She broke away from my neck. Warm blood from the wound slipped into the well of my clavicle, then down my chest. Megan's eyes burned with energy, as if we were on stage, the crowd cheering, the music between us powerful and true. *United.*

She lowered her face, lapping at my clavicle, sucking up the blood caught there, her lips cold against my fevered skin.

Megan turned her attention to the door. She stood quickly, releasing me. Waves of want pulsed off of her. *I can feel her.*

Pearl stood in the doorway, her pale eyes delighted. "You look beautiful, so bloody," she said, her voice warm. "I'm sorry to interrupt, but your father needs to see you, Megan." Pearl glanced at me. "She's about to bleed out."

Megan turned to me. "Oh, God, I'm so sorry."

I looked down at myself. The white robe was soaked with bright red blood. I lifted my hand to touch the puncture but Megan stopped me, taking hold of my wrist. My pulse beat against her strong, cold fingers. She leaned forward and licked the wound; it tingled, then felt tight, like a scar.

"Thank you," she whispered into my ear before standing. "I have to go."

"Wait, Megan." I grabbed at her hand before she could walk away. "Please let me go home. I need to be alone. I need to think." I glanced down at my blood-stained clothing. "This is all so confusing. I feel…so strange."

She pursed her lips and shook her head. "It's not safe."

"Let Darling go home," came a voice from the door. I looked over and saw Megan's father leaning against the frame, Pearl standing behind him, watching us over his shoulder.

"But if she is bitten by a zombie—" Megan said.

"Then her decision will be made," he said, cutting her off. "Dimitri will take her. Megan, come with us now."

She stepped toward him, as if pulled, but turned to me before continuing. "Please," she begged. "Don't go. For me."

I'd never refused Megan anything. Our entire relationship I'd worshiped her, wanting only her happiness and comfort. *To nourish her.*

Should I just stay here and do that? "I can't, Megan—I have to think without influence." Tears choked me, grief cracking through the calm. "I'm so sorry I couldn't save you." *She died. My best friend died. But still lives.*

My head seared with pain, and I closed my eyes. The tourniquet tightened, easing the pain and stilling my thoughts.

"Now." Her father's voice pulled Megan away from me. She stumbled toward him and they left, the door still open to the hall.

I don't know how long I sat there before Dimitri showed up. "She fed from you," he said from the door.

I looked up at him, the world fuzzy.

"Dimitri," I whispered.

"She took too much." He blurred across the room, stopping in front of me.

"I can handle it," I said. *Who is he to tell me my best friend is a bad vampire? Arrogant, sexy, dead man.* I hiccuped a laugh.

"You can't handle it. You are a human. Weak and fragile."

I looked up at him, hardening my gaze. "You don't know me."

A smile twisted his lips, but it did not extend to his eyes. "Megan is young and does not know how to keep you. If you were mine, I'd never let this happen."

I tried to stand, to show him I wasn't some weak little human, but I didn't get far. He caught me, his face suddenly close. He was looking at my neck. "She left a mark." He shook his head. "Such a shame."

"It's none of your concern."

"Calm down," he said, and I instantly felt numb again.

"Boring," I said.

His eyes leaped to mine, his brows rising. "Boring?"

"This numbness you're giving me," I said, his lips close to mine. "It's boring."

"What would you like?" he asked, a sly smile crossing his lips. I didn't answer, just looked at his mouth, remembering how good it felt to suck on his lips.

His influence receded, seeming to flow out of me, and in its wake my own emotions tumbled out, tearing through me, too fast, too many. I squeezed my eyes shut, pain crashing over me. "Is that boring?" he asked, his voice laced with amusement.

"It hurts," I choked.

"How very human of you."

"Fuck you," I gritted, trying to push away from him, but he held me tight, his fingers wrapped around my arms.

"You need a bath." He swung me up into his arms, cradling me like a child. I didn't fight him. Hot tears pooled in my eyes and started down my cheeks. I turned my face into his chest and let the sobs come. "Shh," he said. "If you're going to cry like this, how will I trust you with your own feelings?" He shook his head. "If you were mine, this would not be so."

"I wish I was mine," I said into his chest, my fingers bunching in his shirt.

He stopped, and I felt him looking down at me. I peeked a glance at him, sniffling. His eyes flashed gray, and he licked his lips. "What did you say?" he asked, his voice low. I didn't answer. "You wish you were mine?" His voice filled with something that sounded a lot like hope.

"I wish I was *mine*," I said. "That I belonged to *me*."

His lips tightened, and his eyes shuttered. "This is the wrong world for that."

Hunger thrummed through me, and I reached up, as if a force field pulled me, and ran my fingers into his hair. Dimitri's grip grew tighter as his lips reached mine. A leap of energy jumped from him to me. I pulled back—wanting to see him, hoping to understand what was happening. Lust and confusion warred in his expression. "What are you doing?" he asked. "You are Megan's."

"No, Dimitri. *I'm mine.*"

He kissed me, squeezing me tight against his chest, so that I could barely breathe. *He can crush me.* Dimitri's strength was such that he could crack my bones, press the air out of my lungs, murder me with one embrace. That thought sent zings of lust through me.

His influence floated over my skin, entering me, taking away the confusion and shame I usually felt while in the arms of a man. *But he isn't a man.* I couldn't suck the life out of him. *It is already gone.*

That fear I'd hidden in the back of my mind came up to the front and spread wings, stretching in the space left by that tourniquet. *I'm afraid that I kill anyone who touches me…my foster father, Megan…that I steal their lives and make them mine.*

A part of my psychosis, solved now in the arms of a vampire?

Dimitri groaned against my lips and pulled away from me. "Take me back to the bed," I said. His hair floated around his head he moved so fast. The sensation of unnatural speed, in his arms, felt totally right.

Dimitri slowed, laying me on the blanket with reverence, his weight suspended above me. His eyes—so blue, so pale, so cold and yet so hot—searched my face. I cupped his cheek, pulling him closer.

The vampire did not resist. And when our lips touched, I breathed in, and that current of energy flowed between us, strong and nourishing.

He found my breasts and released a low guttural groan, human in its desperation. "My God," he whispered, "you are not like any other woman I've ever touched." He spoke against my neck as he kissed down toward my breasts, following the trail of dried blood.

He pulled the nightshirt down, his lips soft and warm. His fangs scraped against sensitive flesh. I bowed up toward the incredible touch. His tongue swirled, rough and tantalizing. His hand traveled down my body, fingers playing over my skin before wrapping around my thigh. Then he paused.

Dimitri slowly, luxuriously, let his fingers slide closer, so that I moaned and pressed myself against him. "Impatient?" he mumbled against my breast.

"I need you." *It is true.* There was *something* I needed from him. I'd never accepted how much I needed this, but now it seemed obvious—like when the chorus to a song evades me until it pops right into my head. My whole life, a part of me had been cut off. I'd been afraid of my own nature… my own power. But I could feel it now, hovering in the near distance. Waiting for me to claim it.

Dimitri moaned against my skin, his lips traveling down. His fingers crept closer to my center, and I arched uncontrollably. His palm flattened on my stomach, holding me down. Desire spiked as he blew gently between my thighs. Sweat broke out on my brow even as goose bumps rose across my sensitized flesh.

I want him so badly. It felt like there would never be an end to this torture. And then his mouth was closer, his lips just touching me. *So soft. So good.*

I reached out with my mind, urging him on, urging him to end this ache inside of me, and suddenly, almost as if I'd made it happen, his mouth was on mine, and I could taste myself, and I lost all control. I yanked at his shirt, needing him naked, his smooth, hard flesh pressed against me.

He pulled me to the end of the bed as if I'd commanded him. *Take me now!* Dimitri followed my command. Pain and pleasure twisted into pure power.

He stared at the connection between us, his face unreadable, a stone sculpture, his carved chest rising and falling with labored breaths. *I thought he didn't breathe.* I leaned my head back and closed my eyes.

I wanted more, faster and harder. *All of him.* I could never get enough —there was no amount of *this* that I could not take. That I could not absorb. Each thrust filled me with energy, so that I felt totally alive. *So powerful.*

His influence curled around mine, looking for ways in, for what I wanted. *Who is controlling who?* Keeping my eyes closed, I pictured what I wanted: for him to pick me up, throw me up against a wall, and give me the explosions of satisfaction that I knew would come.

His arms were suddenly around me, and then my back struck the wall, my head cradled by his strong hand—keeping me safe. Dimitri pressed himself up against me, his body solid, perfect, hard and thrusting. My legs wrapped around his waist. Energy built in me. I breathed him in, and he let me. He would let me take everything from him. Dimitri offered it…*enjoyed* it.

I hold the power.

My orgasm ripped through me, and he broke the kiss, his eyes flashing gray and ice blue as he watched me. The wild pleasure seemed to go on and on. The speed at which he'd brought me to it, compared to the length of the experience, made me feel as though time was no longer what I'd believed it to be. *Nothing is as I believed it to be.*

He looked at me confused, pained, out of control...or under mine? His fangs out, pressing into his bottom lip, he kept moving into me. I felt his influence as he tried to turn my head and expose my neck. But I didn't want him to bite me. "No," I whispered. "Come without it." His body shuddered, and with one final thrust, he pushed himself deep inside of me, and his body shook. Dimitri pressed his lips to mine, the link between us a burning line of power.

He pulled back. There was a flush to his cheeks, his eyes gray, bright, human almost. My heart pounded against my ribs, pumping blood through my veins at incredible speed. I reached up and touched his face, and I felt that beat, that thump, leap into him. Dimitri flinched away, and when he looked back, his eyes were cold again. Ice blue and empty. "What did you just do?" His voice held the menace of a cornered predator.

CHAPTER SEVENTEEN

Energy vibrated through my entire body as Dimitri lowered the hood over my face. Wrapping my arms around myself, I closed my eyes behind the blindfold. The car rumbled to life. The wheels crunched over gravel and then we were on paved roads, the car humming along. *Going home.*

I wore a pair of sweatpants and a T-shirt that belonged to Megan, and I could smell her on them. And that wasn't the only thing I could smell. I could smell my sweat on Dimitri's skin—even though we'd both showered. I could smell the night—the animals that lived in the forest, the flowers that bloomed in the dark, the soil, the rot, the life…everything.

The Universe sings a song, and I can hear it.

I'd watched Dimitri dress, a rapt audience enthralled by the show. *He really did move like a dancer—all controlled energy and elegant lines.*

The vampire wore a pale blue collared shirt, just a shade lighter than his eyes. Eyes that kept wandering to me as he changed, flashing gray in the warm light of his bedroom. *Dimitri's bedroom.* If my room had been built for a princess in a tower, his belonged to the master of a castle. It was in a turret. An honest to God turret, with windows all the way around.

His closet was as large as my bedroom at home, and I'd watched him dress through the open door. A linen three-piece suit. *Who even wears a three-piece suit?* Dimitri the vampire, that's who—the most statuesque and elegant thing I'd ever seen.

I took in a deep breath, the fabric of the hood brushing my lips, desire stirring at the memory of him buttoning that vest, his eyes pinning me.

Dimitri laid a hand on my thigh, and I instantly felt calmer—and duller. "Stop it," I said through the hood.

"But I like to touch you."

"Just don't try to control me." *Said the chicken to the fox.*

He huffed a small laugh but did ease off. "How can you control my emotions?" I asked.

"It is impossible to explain to you."

"Try me."

Dimitri squeezed my thigh, his fingers burning. I put my hand over his, and he turned his palm so that our fingers could lace. "Pearl said you can control your own emotions and in time learn to control others."

"It is something like that."

"Come on, Dimitri. If I'm supposed to be considering becoming a vampire, I'd like a little more information."

He didn't speak for a long moment. I held my breath, waiting. "First, tell me how you did what you did." His voice sounded almost unsure.

"Did what?"

"Made me *feel*." His voice was so low I could hardly hear it over the tires whining over blacktop.

Something clicked in my brain. *They can't love or feel like me.* "How can Megan still love me?" I asked.

"What do you mean?" His voice held a subtle tremor.

"She still loves me, but you can't love. Vampires can't love."

"Are you so sure she loves you?" His voice was haughty—as if I was a smitten foolish girl.

"Yes," I answered, totally sure. "I could see it in her eyes, feel it against my skin, sense it in the path of her tongue on my skin, divine it from the crushing pull of her fangs—" *I can feel his emotions, too.* They whispered against my flesh, filled the space around us. And then I felt mine, weighted by his. And it was clear to me, in a single moment—I could see it all right in front of my blindfolded eyes, like a glowing map.

His emotions were a cloudy white mist all around us. Mine were a hot little ball of red at the center of me—right in my pelvis. I just had to stay there, and he'd never find me. No one would. *I've hidden for over a decade— safe in my center.*

We drove in silence as I stared at this new landscape, stunned I'd never seen it before.

"Megan can't sing anymore, can she?" I asked.

"I don't know."

He is lying. I felt the lie on my skin, the brush of it against the fine hairs on my arm. Saw the way the mist shifted to obscure the truth.

"You can take off your hood." *He wants to distract me.* "We are far enough from the house. And besides, you've got one of the worst senses of direction I've ever seen. You couldn't find your way back there with a map," he said with a small chuckle, taking his hand off my leg. I felt anger at him. It was the first emotion to explode when given the space. I saw it like a rocket, arching out of me.

I pulled the hood off, turning to him. "What do you know about my sense of direction?" Before he could answer, I saw that the car was enveloped in smoke. "What is going on?" I turned in my seat, scanning the area.

"Fires," he said. "This part of the city is burning." He cleared his throat. "We kept you sleeping for a week. It's been busy."

A zombie came through the smoke, stumbling, half its face a gory mess, the other half splattered with blood, the one remaining eye swiveling in its socket. It stepped into our path and Dimitri swung around it. I watched as the creature swiveled and, arms outstretched, began to stumble after us. Soon it was invisible in the thick smoke.

"All this in just a week?" I asked.

"Sometimes the world changes in an instant."

"Yes," I agreed, thinking of my father's death and how my reality shifted. I ran my hand over where the wolf bit me as I tried to save his life. It had healed by the time they opened the cabinet. The tears in my clothing remained, but underneath, my skin was smooth.

Dimitri placed his hand on my thigh again. "I'm okay," I said.

"I told you, I like touching you."

The smoke thinned revealing abandoned streets. "Are they evacuating the city?"

"Quite the opposite," Dimitri said. "They are quarantining it."

"Will that help?"

"Nothing will help."

I turned in my seat again, staring around, trying to figure out where we were. I recognized the street, but without people, it seemed foreign, like we were in a different world. Dimitri took a left, and I recognized the block—it usually bustled with people. Today, it was clogged with cars, their lights turned off, empty, blocking the street. Dimitri eased up behind them and then pulled to a stop. "We'll have to walk from here."

"Okay," I took off my seat belt. "Why would people just leave their cars?" Dimitri looked over at me, his eyes unfocused as he stared at me. "What?" I asked.

"I'm not sure," he answered, leaning toward me. He sniffed my hair. "There is something about you...I can't..." He shook his head, a brief expression of frustration crossing his brow.

I reached into the back seat for my violin. "I need to go home," I said, pressing my will against his.

He touched my cheek as I pulled the violin toward me, just a slight brush of his warm fingers against my skin before he turned to his door. Instantly, he was opening mine and offering his hand. I took it and stood.

Dimitri turned suddenly—a zombie appeared from the smoke, staggering toward us on unsteady legs. Once a man, the figure was bloated, the buttons on its shirt straining, his neck grotesquely mauled, part of his lips devoured. Dimitri grabbed it—the zombie struggled against him, straining its tongue toward me.

With what seemed like no effort at all, Dimitri dug his fingers into the zombie's scalp, turning it into a horrific bowling ball. I watched with fascinated horror as Dimitri pulled straight up, ripping the head loose from the neck. The body fell to the ground and Dimitri turned to me, the head in his hand, its jaw still working.

"There is only one way to kill a zombie," Dimitri said, as if we were suddenly in a civics class. "The heart does not matter." He held out his other hand, which grasped a still heart in it. Blood and gore dripped between his fingers around it.

I swallowed down bile. Dimitri then held up the head with its animated features. "The brain," he said. "You must pierce the brain." I stared at the head. "Darling," Dimitri said, his voice low. "Kill it." I looked up at him. He smiled at me encouragingly. "You can do it," he said with a nod. I didn't move. Dimitri frowned.

"With what?" I asked.

"There is a knife in the glove box."

I put the violin down at my feet and reached back into the car. A hunting knife sat where you'd expect to find registration papers. Its blade was curved, the handle black and indented with finger grips. I turned back to Dimitri, holding the knife, my fingers relaxed, the way my father taught me.

"You don't need to worry about me," I told Dimitri.

"Let's see you kill this thing, then."

The head in his hand clapped its teeth together. Sirens wailed in the distance. I turned toward the sound but saw only smoke billowing from behind us. "Darling," Dimitri said, and I felt his will upon me, like a warm blanket wrapping around me. "Kill it," he said, his voice harsher than before, his fangs distending slightly. "It's not a person anymore. Whatever was human about it is gone."

I chewed on my bottom lip, knowing he told the truth but uncomfortable driving a knife into an animated head. *Call me crazy, but that just seems wrong.*

Dimitri stepped closer, dropping the rotting heart onto the ground and holding the decapitated head up in front of me. Its lips, at least what remained of them, pulled back from its teeth as it tried to reach me. "This thing will kill you."

"Take me home." I put a note of pleading into my voice. "I need to think. I'm confused by what is happening; I'm sorry." I could feel him trying to enter me, his mind probing and hungry for control.

Dimitri smiled. "You don't control me, girl," he said, dropping the head and crushing it under his foot, without taking his pale blue eyes off of mine.

He pulled a packet of wet wipes from inside his jacket pocket and cleaned his hands. *This man is prepared for the zombie apocalypse.*

"What are you?" he asked, hands cleaned, wipe dropped carelessly onto the ground. *Littering is the least of the world's problems right now, I guess.*

He growled. And suddenly his hands held either side of my face, my back pressed up against the car. His fangs descended. "What are you doing to me? I must kiss you." His eyes narrowed. "I have not felt for so long…what are you?" he hissed, his pupils large and black.

A scream tore through the air. It was coming from a three-story brick building, its balconies filled with blooming flowers that didn't seem to know the world was ending. "Help!" a woman sobbed.

"We have to help her," I said to Dimitri. His gaze did not shift, just continued to stare at me. Almost like he was mesmerized. "Please." The scream grew louder, more desperate. I brought my hand up and wrapped it around his wrist.

He grunted, bent down, and picked up my violin, then gripped me roughly around the waist, crouching before launching us up onto the balcony. We landed lightly on the far side of the plants. I slid down his body, slowly, like he was taking his time letting me go.

Long white curtains shrouded the interior, but another scream urged me forward. Dimitri held me back. "Wait here." He placed my violin on the ground.

"I'm trained in first aid," I answered.

"Stay." His voice rooted me to the floor. Dimitri blurred through the curtains, leaving them lifted in his wake. Before they fell back into place I saw a young boy, maybe seven or eight, curled behind a couch, his hands over his ears, eyes squeezed shut, tears running down his face.

I fought to take a step but my feet would not budge from the balcony's wood floor. Dimitri's influence grounded me to the spot. Another scream—short and desperate.

I closed my eyes and found the tendrils of power Dimitri used to hold me in place. Taking a deep breath, I plucked at them with my mind. My feet came loose and I stumbled forward, reaching out for the curtains to catch myself.

I grabbed at the cloth but instead of stopping my fall, the whole fixture ripped out of the wall, bringing the bar and both curtains down on top of me as I fell into the apartment. *Here I come to save the day!*

I hit the floor wrapped up in the curtains. Strong hands lifted me, all the spots where I'd fallen no longer hurting. The cloth disappeared, and Dimitri stood over me. "You are okay," he told me. I nodded, agreeing. "Sorry that you fell. That shouldn't have been possible."

"I'm fine." I tried to disentangle myself from him, not wanting to admit what I'd done. He let go of me reluctantly and I stepped around him to where the boy rocked back and forth, his eyes still squeezed shut, hands over his ears. I crouched down in front of him and placed a hand gently on his forearm. He flinched and turned away without opening his eyes.

Dimitri came up behind me, and I could see his cloud of influence envelop the child. He dropped his hands looking up at Dimitri with red-rimmed eyes. "Boy, are you bitten?" Dimitri asked him. He shook his head. "Good," Dimitri said. "You will live for now then."

"What about my mom and dad?" he asked, his voice high but calm.

"Your father is dead."

"My mother?"

Dimitri turned back into the room and asked. "Are you bit?"

I looked over the top of the couch. A woman leaned against the wall, her jeans and T-shirt spattered in blood, her hair half in a pony-tail and half out. Next to her lay the headless body of a man. She looked up at Dimitri. "Yes," she answered, her voice vibrating with shock.

Dimitri turned back to the boy. "If I do not kill her now, she will become a zombie, just like your father did."

"No!" The boy said, standing up, reaching his hands out, pleading with the vampire. "I want her to live."

"Not possible."

"Dimitri," I said. "Can't something be done? Shouldn't we take her to the hospital?"

"They would shoot her. The army is there. Crescent City is under martial law. They are trying to save the world, Darling. This woman's life means nothing to them." He looked down at me. *It means nothing to him, too.*

"Can you turn her into a vampire?" I asked.

He stepped back as if I'd slapped him. "No." His voice came out flat —past anger to something else.

"Why not?" I pushed.

"You do not know what you ask."

"There is nothing we can do?"

"We can offer her mercy, Darling. Killing her before she becomes a zombie is mercy." Dimitri cocked his head and listened. "We must go."

In a flash he was across the room, his hands on the woman's head, and then a crack. He dropped her, and she slumped on the ground. Then he was back at my side. "Come," he said.

"What about him?" I asked, my voice high with panic.

Dimitri leaned down to the boy. "Men in uniforms are coming," he said. "Tell them that you have not been bitten. They will care for you." He placed a hand on the boy's shoulder. "Your parents loved you. They want you to live. Be brave, boy."

Dimitri's arm wrapped around my waist, and he pressed me against his body. "Wait," I said, everything moving too fast. "We can't just leave him!" Dimitri stepped out onto the balcony and looked down.

I followed his gaze. Dark green trucks with white stenciled writing drove down the block, heading toward the blockade of cars that had stopped us. Behind them smoke continued to grow thicker, the smell a horrible mix of building materials, chemicals, plastic, and something... almost like barbecue. *Dear God, that smell is people. I am smelling people burning.*

Dimitri tightened his grip, snatched up my violin then jumped, landing us on the roof. He hooked his arm under my knees so that he held me like a child.

Dimitri took off in the direction of my house. He ran so fast that I had to turn my face into his chest to keep the wind from blinding me.

CHAPTER EIGHTEEN

DIMITRI GLANCED over the edge of the roof and I followed his gaze seeing my balcony below. There were no cars in the streets, no green trucks. "They are doing door-to-door searches," he said. "They have cleared your building already. You will be relatively safe here as long as you don't let anyone in."

He leaped down onto my balcony, landing in a crouch. "Do you have food and fresh water?" he asked as he let me down.

I took my violin from him, nodding. "Thanks for bringing me home," I said, opening my door.

"Will you invite me in?" he asked.

"Do you need an invitation?" I leaned against the door jamb, watching him. *Is it true vampires can't enter your house unless they are invited?*

"It is considered polite to wait for one." His voice was soft, the white mist of his influence swirling around us both, brushing up against me, feathering over my hair and skin, soothing away any anxieties.

"I need to think without you controlling me," I sighed.

"I understand." He stepped closer to me. "But, Darling, I don't need an invitation to influence you. I could do it from across the world." He closed the distance between us, the fog of his aura pushing into my apartment as his fangs began to descend.

Desire spiraled up from the hot red center of me.

His eyes lit, and he growled, "Invite me in."

"Please come in."

Dimitri stepped through the open door, pushing me into the apartment and closed it behind him. He took my violin from me, placing it on the floor then wrapped his arms around me and pressed his lips against mine. Lifting me, he carried me to the couch.

"I will drink from you." He kissed down my chin. I leaned back, and he nipped gently where Megan had bitten me. A shiver ran through my body.

"I don't think so," I said, my voice sounding unsure and confused. My breath was shallow, body vibrating. "You shouldn't use your influence to convince me to give you my blood," I said.

"I'm not," he said against my skin, his hands roaming over my body. "I think you are influencing me." He grew still.

"What?" I asked.

He raised his head, looking at me. "That is impossible," he said. "It...you. Are you a witch?"

I laughed. The look on his face was priceless—Dimitri, strong, ancient, cocky, predator Dimitri, all confused and adorable. "A witch? No." I shook my head. "I'm just a fiddle player."

His eyes narrowed, sparking hot blue. "No, you are much more than that." He stood and walked away from me. "I don't understand." He glanced back, as if he didn't have a choice, as if the red rock of heat at my center drew him. "How is this possible?"

"What?" I sat up, wanting the weight of him back on me. He bit his lip. "What's wrong?" I asked.

"You cannot stay here." He shook his head. "It is far too dangerous. Brad was wrong to let you return."

"Unless he wants me to die," I said.

Dimitri shook his head. "No, you are of his blood. He wants you to turn."

"Why?"

"The more of your blood that is turned, the more powerful you are."

"So why don't they just use their influence and turn me without my consent?"

"You would not be a very good vampire then. Those who do not want to turn often die in the process. You must want eternal life, be willing to give things up for it." Dimitri looked up then. He sniffed the air. "Emmanuel," he said, his voice strange. There was an emotion in his tone I could not discern.

"What? How do you know Emmanuel?"

"He is coming," Dimitri said, ignoring my question. *Right, Dimitri stalked me—that's how he knows my bassist.*

Dimitri blurred out onto the balcony, and I followed him. Emmanuel's rusted red truck pulled over in front of my building. I ran back toward the front door. Dimitri followed, and as I reached for the knob, my body froze in place. "He is bitten," Dimitri said. "You cannot let him in."

"Let go of me!" I struggled against the force that held me—thick, white cords of power wrapped around my arms and legs, tethering me to Dimitri.

"Stop fighting me," he said.

"I want—" I began but Dimitri sucked my will from me. I saw it leave like a cloud of dust punched from a long abandoned pillow. I slumped against the binds that held me, the white tentacles wrapping around me like vines. *If he releases me now, I'll crumple to the floor.*

That lack of will, the complete loss of all I'd wanted the moment ago, brought tears to my eyes. A deep hopelessness seeped into my bones.

"Darling!" Emmanuel knocked at my door, his voice strained. Dimitri moved my body forward, placing my eye so that I could see out the peep-hole. *See,* I heard Dimitri's voice inside my head. *He is gone.* Emmanuel, his curls damp with sweat, brown eyes strained with pain, his neck…his beautiful neck, badly mauled.

He coughed violently, and blood hit the eye of my peephole, leaving it dark. *If you let him in, he'll kill you.*

"Darling, please. We need to talk."

"I can't," I heard myself say. "You've been bitten."

Emmanuel banged on the door. "Please trust me," he said. He coughed again, and I heard him lean his weight against the door. "I'll come back," he wheezed. "Don't leave. Stay here. I'll come back for you."

His footsteps stumbled away. Dimitri released me, the slick white vines of his mind uncurling. My will vacuumed back into me. I ran to my balcony, watching the empty street below.

Dimitri came to stand next to me. He laid his hand on my back, a warm, calming balm. Emmanuel fell out the door, stumbled off the side-walk and landed in the street, his whole body violently shaking. "He's seizing," I said.

"The final stage before he turns," Dimitri answered.

I can't help in any way. My heart thudded in my chest.

It was agonizing minutes before Emmanuel stopped shaking. He slowly climbed to his feet. His head swiveled, first looking one way then the other. He started off to the south, toward the fire, his steps no longer human, his gait the shuffling and disjointed march of the dead.

"Have you been with him?" Dimitri asked. I didn't answer, just watched Emmanuel's stilted walk. "Answer me," Dimitri commanded.

"We just kissed." Melancholy weighed down my words so that I whispered.

"You are his?" Dimitri asked, his voice soft.

I shook my head. *I am no one's.*

Dimitri straightened, his hand leaving my back. "Brad commanded that I leave you here, and so I will. But in twenty-four hours I will be back." He turned me to him and caressed my cheek. I leaned into his touch, the warm mist of his influence petting me. Dimitri's eyes flashed gray for a second before he turned away.

Jumping off my balcony, he blurred from sight. With him went his influence, and for the first time since seeing Megan again, my emotions were my own.

I felt too much. A crippling tsunami of feelings wracked through me —grief, fear, rage. Clutching at the railing of my balcony, I fell to my knees. My fingers gave out and I collapsed, rolling into the fetal position.

Sobs tore through me. *I may never breathe again.* Colors flashed behind my closed lids. I bit down on my lip, trying to pull myself back— searching for that girl who fought a wolf. Searching for my father's daughter.

He was real and so was she.

I could almost hear my father's voice. *"What do we do when we fall down, Darling?"*

"We get back up," I ground out through the sobs, fighting the spasms, concentrating on evening my breathing. It was real, I knew that now. All my memories of him. Of the life we'd shared. All the things that for years, *for years*, I'd tried to forget, ignore, and deny, had been let loose.

I remembered my father's voice. And it urged me on.

Using the railing, I pulled myself up and swiped at my face, wiping away the tears.

It was all quiet below, the street usually packed with musicians, tourists and locals lay deathly still in night. Not even the stray cats prowled.

I stood there, gaining control of myself, finding that red glowing center and listening to my heartbeat. *I am alive. And I plan to stay that way.*

Walking back into the apartment, I closed and locked the balcony doors behind me.

A note waited on the refrigerator. Written in neat black handwriting, it read:

Dear Darling,

I hope that you receive this letter. Please try to call me. Phones will probably be out soon, but it's worth a try. If you cannot reach me by phone, please try me at the hospital. If the hospital has fallen, go to 67 Adam's Way.
They can help you. Explain that I sent you.

It is vitally important that you reach me, Darling. Try to find me. Use your strength.

I have information about your father, but more importantly, I think that you can save the world.

Dr. Issa Tor

Save the world my ass.
Dr. Issa Tor was as crazy as me.
But it turns out I'm not so crazy.

Leaving the note on the fridge, I went to my closet and pulled out my suitcase and a rack of shoes to get to the back panel. I banged on the upper left-hand corner, and it popped open. Inside were two bows, one child-sized and the other meant for an adult.

They'd been in that kitchen cabinet with me along with a leather quiver for my arrows that I'd worn on my back.

I had clutched onto the smooth wood while the social worker told me my father was just a figment of my imagination, that my life up until the moment I met her was all just a "coping mechanism." Then she informed me the bows belonged to the dead man in the apartment where they found me and that I had to give them up.

Megan helped me get them back. We filed paperwork and made phone calls. Eventually, they were located, and my identity confirmed as the little girl found at that horrific scene. We paid for the shipping, and when they arrived in Crescent City, I put them in my closet—hid them away just like my memories, just like that red spark at the center of me. Megan bought arrows and tried to get me to teach her but I refused.

Dr. Issa Tor had promised me information about my father, but I didn't need it. No one knew him like I did.

I brought out my father's bow first. Used for hunting deer, it was armed with knife-tipped arrows, the kind that could strike straight to a deer's heart, or a zombie's brain, I figured.

I blew dust off its gleaming wooden handle and checked to make sure it was still in order before placing it on my bed. Pulling out the smaller bow, I turned it. Really, it was more my size than the one my father had used, but its wooden-tipped arrows might not be that useful.

I placed it next to the larger one and looked down at them for a moment. The sun rose, casting a warm glow through the window as I stood there. I wanted to go back to the cemetery, find that Suki creature and ask her some questions. But figured I'd have a better chance of finding her at sunset than sunrise—that's when I'd seen her before.

I put on yoga pants and a snug T-shirt, both black. I tied my hair into a tight bun.

I wanted to arrive at the cemetery as the day turned to night. *I should rest.* But my mind raced, and my emotions burned.

Reading Issa's note again, I picked up my phone, but the lines were dead. I'd deal with him later...after I'd talked to Suki again. *All of this is real.*

I turned to my violin case, almost afraid to open it and find my instrument crushed. But there it was, its same gleaming self. Picking it up, I knew what would come out. I could feel the need to play; my hands shook, but they would steady against the strings. Pulling out the bow, its familiar shape helped to ground me.

Closing my eyes, I laid it to the strings and pulled, letting out a low chord, dark and sad. Back again, and I went up a chord, hearing the sound vibrating through the violin, into my chin, down my neck, and hitting me in the heart, echoing what I felt there. Then I was off, playing so hard that hair escaped from my well-placed bun, flopping over my face, dancing with the sounds that I made.

It was a song that Megan and I wrote soon after moving to Crescent City. It stayed a favorite not only of ours but also of our fans in the following ten years. I hadn't played it since she disappeared, but now it came out of me like water rushing over a fall, landing into a fathomless pond and bubbling against the shore.

The song ended with Megan a cappella, singing the chorus again. As I stilled my bow, I could almost hear her. *"Father, forgive my sins, and let me in. Let me in."*

CHAPTER NINETEEN

I LEFT AN HOUR BEFORE SUNSET, my father's bow and a quiver full of arrows slung across my back, my child size one bungeed to the rear of my bike. Using a leather belt, I'd fashioned a holder for two of our kitchen knives, one on each hip. Around my waist I'd secured a thick chain and lock.

I walked out to the balcony and looked up and down the street before heading downstairs. A grocery bag floated on the breeze, making the wind's whims obvious to me. The smoke from the fires was headed north, along with the white plastic bag. I took a deep breath, smelling that toxic mix of burning buildings and meat.

I pushed my bike out of the doorway, searching up and down again before climbing on. I stayed in the center of the road so that I could see into each doorway and behind every car. The bars that usually would be full of early drinkers sat empty, doors locked and windows boarded.

Were people inside? Hiding from the death that wandered the streets? Or perhaps they'd all been rounded up. Maybe they would be safe...

How many people would the vampires take to their camps? How many would be okay with it, and how many would fight? Would death by vampire feel as good as Megan's taking from me? Better?

I shuddered at the memory, a mix of want and revulsion clouding my thoughts.

A thud drew my attention. What was once a woman walked repeatedly into a door. I pedaled faster, trying to put distance between me and the zombie, my heart beating faster as my legs pumped. I turned and had to brake hard—about ten zombies swayed in the middle of the block. I backed up slowly.

One spotted me and started forward. Its momentum built and speed increased. The others followed. I tore my eyes off of them and turned the bike, pedaling hard, fear pushing me forward.

I could hear them behind me, some of them moaning, all of them hurrying, their footsteps heavy on the pavement that I cruised over.

I took a sharp left and skid to a stop. Another herd of zombies hunched over a bloody pile. The smell coming off of them tickled my jaw, and I swallowed back bile. The moaning behind me was getting closer.

I took to the sidewalk and pedaled faster, standing up, pushing forward. *I'll have to ride right by them.*

I flew past with my heart in my throat and legs burning with effort.

Glancing back, I saw the group following me come around the corner and run into them—they fell, going down in a big tangled mess of bloody limbs and soulless eyes.

I focused in front of me. *I need to get to the cemetery.* I turned left, working my way toward it but a woman's scream slowed me. "Help!" she begged, drawing my eyes to an open door. Behind me, a few zombies turned the corner, their arms outstretched toward me.

I couldn't ignore her plea and veered to the opening, riding right into the room.

The darkness blinded me.

A small man, or what was left of him, knocked me off my bike. I kicked out and he fell back, but only for a moment. He lunged again. My left leg was tangled under my bike, but I kicked hard with my right, sending him off me long enough to grab the knife from my hip. I held it up and the creature dove, stabbing itself in the eye.

I pushed him away with the hilt of the knife and stumbled to my feet, grabbing for the door.

A zombie, her face pale and bloated, reached out to me but I slammed it, leaning against the wood. The thud of her body ricocheted through to me.

I grabbed a chair and pushed it under the knob. Then I stepped away slowly, the door shaking on its hinges as the group of zombies pressed forward.

They don't give up. Just like death.

I scanned the dim interior, my eyes more adjusted now. There was a low stage and just a couple of tables—I knew this place; it was small but got wild. Loud and raucous, it was an awesome place to gig…or it had been.

Legs stuck out from behind the wooden bar. I circled around slowly. I recognized a waitress—I couldn't remember her name, but she always gave me a warm smile and had an easy laugh.

Her throat was ripped out, now. *She will never laugh again.* My stomach dropped. *I have to pierce her brain. Can't let her change.*

I knelt down and felt for a pulse at her wrist. She was warm, but there was no heartbeat. Walking back over to the dead zombie, I pulled my knife from his eye and approached the body. I took a deep breath before plunging it into her. *I'd want someone to do the same for me.*

I went out the back door—it opened up to a deserted alley. Riding my bike slowly to the edge of the street, I peered around the corner toward the front entrance. Around twenty zombies pressed against the door of the bar.

I turned away from them and continued toward the cemetery. The sun hovered low in the sky now, and I wanted to get there before it turned the world pink and soft. Twilight seemed the best time to reach Suki— when the world was neither light nor dark but dreamy and filled with shadows.

I have some questions for that apparition.

When I rode through the cemetery gates, I threw my bike down, dashed back to the entrance, and, grabbing the two halves of the gate, slammed them together with a clang that echoed among the mausoleums. Taking the chain and lock from around my waist, I circled it through each door of the gate, the metal banging together, knocking off bits of the old black paint. I secured the chain with the lock and then turned back to my bike and the rest of the cemetery, pulling my bow off my back and raising it up to my eye.

Left, right, both aisles were clear and quiet. The mausoleums looked undisturbed, like no one had been here and nobody cared: crumbling walls, patches of grass growing everywhere they could. *Life doesn't give up that easy.* There must be some way to stop this madness.

I edged forward, moving around my bike, looking down the barrel of my bow. Reaching the next path, I pressed my back against the mausoleum to my left and listened hard. I could hear sirens far in the distance but nothing close.

One quick step out in the aisle looking left—clear—spinning, crouching, looking right. A figure turned toward me. Its sandy blonde hair fell down its back to just above its shoulder blades. It wore a pink shirt with a collar and khaki shorts. The zombie turned slowly, its body leaning to one side, hunched and unnatural.

I waited for it to face me, sweat running down my back, my breath shallow. Its gaze was down, bangs hanging over it. The dead woman raised her head, eyes glowing an eerie green in the half light. I pulled the trigger, and the zombie's legs buckled. She fell to the ground in a heap of limbs.

I checked behind me quickly, to my right and to my left, then approached it. Bracing my foot against her shoulder, I pulled out my arrow. It made a sickening suction noise as it slid slowly from her skull.

Placing the arrow back in my clip, I held up the bow again. The sun sank lower, the shadows growing darker as I cleared the rest of the cemetery. I worked my way back to Suki's resting place, stopping in the center aisle to look back at the main gate.

A single zombie stood there. When it saw me, the thing's arms stretched through the gate, fingers kneading at the air, a sob-like sound escaping from its bloated body. It probably died a couple of hours ago—its body was filling with gasses.

Suki's mausoleum was covered in sugar packets, pieces of gum, beads, cash, paper notes, and mini bottles of liquor. I wasn't the only person asking her for answers.

I pulled out a sugar packet from the small pocket of my yoga pants and placed it on the ledge. Using a broken piece of brick, I scratched three question marks into the soft cement of the mausoleum. *Please talk to me.* I closed my eyes, seeing the need radiating out of me behind my lids.

A clang at the gate snapped my eyes open, and I raised the bow with tired arms. I walked to the main aisle and checked the entrance. Now there were four zombies out there, all pressing against the metal. *How many will it take to rip the rusted hinges from the aged cement forming the front wall?*

I turned back to Suki's gravesite and lowered my bow. She wasn't here.

Do I need to cry onto the sugar packet? Or maybe it was the time of day. It was almost dark now, the west horizon bright orange.

The smoke in the south looked like a black storm. The glow from the fire at its base made it almost look like there were two sunsets.

Should I sit down, the way I'd been last time she came? How could I risk resting with those things at the gate?

The sun slipped beneath the horizon, and the soft hues of dusk arrived, settling over the cemetery, making the shift to darkness feel slow and leisurely. Then the light winked out and the cemetery fell dark. With a whirl of electric current, the street lights buzzed to life, illuminating the sidewalks but not penetrating the depths of the cemetery where I waited.

Checking the gate again, I counted ten bodies pressing against it. As I watched, a small figure pushed through the legs of the others and reached its arm through, then a leg. *A child.* Its head got stuck.

I turned away, tears pushing at my eyes. *No time for that now.* How much longer could I wait?

"Hello." I whirled around, bow raised. Suki wore the same outfit as the last time I'd seen her, all white with just the red embroidery on her head scarf. She frowned at me. "Lower that weapon," she said in a voice that seemed to vibrate the air around me. A loose brick in the mausoleum next to me fell, breaking into pieces when it hit the path. I lowered the bow.

Suki turned back to her gravesite, and I followed her. With her back to me, she reached up and placed a candle on the roof of the mausoleum. With a small wave of her hand, the wick flared and then glowed warmly, creating flickering shadows in the narrow space. "That bow is too big for you," she said without turning around.

"What is going on?" I asked. She didn't answer, instead picking up one of the mini bottles of liquor. She twisted off the cap and drank. "Emmanuel is dead." My voice hitched as tears caught in my throat.

Suki picked up my sugar packet, handing it to me. I dabbed at my tears. Her fingers waggled at me, and I handed it back. "Can I help him?" I asked.

She laughed, low and short—a sound that made it clear I didn't know anything—as she placed the sugar packet next to her candle.

When she turned back, a thin, yellow snake slithered around her arms in a figure eight, its corn-colored scales smooth and shining in the light. "You can't help him," she said. "Or yourself."

She stepped forward, the snake speeding up, turning into a blur of light in her arms. "You're no good to anyone." She raised the ball of light and squatted, then pushing hard off her feet, launched the sphere over the graves.

It arched low, lighting the cemetery then dropped by the gate. A hissing started slow but grew louder. I covered my ears and Suki watched me, smiling.

"What are you doing?" I yelled over the sound. Her face darkened, eyebrows inching closer above narrowed eyes. "You're so powerful?" I pointed with one hand, letting the hissing sound batter against me. "What are you going to do about it? How are you going to stop this?"

"Get out!" she said, her voice even louder than the hissing, the buildings around me shaking. "Now!" Her voice knocked into me and I stumbled, hitting a mausoleum hard. "Go!"

I turned and ran to the center aisle. The hissing faded. There were no zombies at the gate. *She destroyed them. How?*

I turned to ask her, but Suki was gone—not even the smoke from her candle remained. *Well that's super freaking useful.*

Jogging down the path, I picked up my bike and looked through the gate, pushing my face so that I could see in both directions. No zombies, no snakes. Unlocking the chain, I wrapped it back around my waist, climbed on my bike, pushed through the gates, and pedaled as fast as I could away from the cemetery and toward the hospital.

How did she get rid of those zombies? I hadn't seen any bodies. She'd made them *disappear.*

I came around a corner and skidded to a stop—zombies filled the street in front of me. The stench of rot and death made me gag.

I turned around, pedaling back the way I'd come, but I'd been spotted.

They filled the space between the buildings, pouring around stopped cars, knocking into pillars, some falling and others climbing over them. A chaotic, determined mob of bloated corpses. They hadn't been dead long. *It all changes in a moment—hints of disaster, then an explosion of chaos.*

I pedaled madly, taking the first turn I could—a zombie stumbled out from behind a car directly in my path. I smashed into it, falling off the bike. It was on me instantly, biting hard into my leg, ripping a scream from me. *No, no, no.*

I should have become a fucking vampire.

The rest of them were right there, stumbling around the corner. Seeing me on the ground excited them. *Their quarry is injured.*

I pulled my bow and killed the one on my leg. I stumbled to my feet, the pain in my calf numbed by the mass of adrenaline pumping into me. Backing away from the herd, I pulled arrows from my quiver in a smooth motion, firing as I went. My arrows found their mark, and I killed two before another reached me.

It grabbed at the bow, and I fired through its mouth. Another latched onto my arm, and its teeth sank into me. I dropped the bow and pulled a knife, thrusting it through the thing's eye. My quiver ripped from my back and teeth sank into my shoulder. Another was on me, my forearm between its teeth. *I'm dying.*

The zombie's head exploded, and I sucked in a breath of surprise. A blur of motion spun through the mob, sending them flying, heads popping, bodies hitting the surrounding buildings hard enough to crack plaster and break windows.

An arm wrapped around my waist, and wind rushed in my ears. We landed on a roof and I looked up—Dimitri laid me down, the black tar still warm from the sun.

Liquid heat pooled under me as I stared up into the dark sky. The stars were falling away from me. *I'm bleeding to death. It's okay. Dimitri will kill me before I become one of the undead.*

The strangled, guttural sounds of frustration from those horrific, plagued creatures reached me from the street.

"Darling." Dimitri held my face, his hands cradling me. His eyes flashed gray as I breathed in. Color rose in his cheeks as I felt that tie between us. He brought his lips to mine. His energy passed through his skin, warming as it passed over my lips and into my bloodstream, searing through my veins, and healing me. Curing me. Feeding me. *Saving me.*

CHAPTER TWENTY

DIMITRI'S KISSES, his whisper-soft touch, and bridled strength—the connection between us—pulled me back together, rid my body of disease, filled my veins with fresh blood...cured me.

I don't know how or why, but it happened.

The rough tar roof scraped against my back. I wrapped my legs around his waist and took and took and took...power coursed through me. The night came alive all around me. The energy's intensity grew—I pushed, rolling us. Dimitri held my hips, his eyes black and fangs long.

I rode him, my head thrown back. He played with me, making me crazy and wild. Blood thundered in my ears, and there was nothing but him and me and the heat between us. *I lost it. Lost everything... but me.*

I collapsed against his chest, my fingers running into his hair, pulling his mouth to mine. *Taking even more.*

He groaned, his hands diving into my long locks. "I'm not done yet," he growled. "I may never be done with you." His voice softened, and he cupped my cheek, looking into my eyes. *The predator is still there but so is a man...a living being.* "I wonder if eternity is long enough." Dimitri's voice faded as he stared into my eyes. Then he leaned forward, kissing me gently, his hips moving slowly under me until I whimpered against him.

He put me on my hands and knees. The uneven texture of the roof felt right, painful almost, against my sensitized skin. "So beautiful," he whispered against my flesh. His hands roamed down my legs. "Your wound," he said. "It's healed."

His palm wrapped around my calf where I'd been bitten. "Yes," I said, my head still light from the force of my pleasure, the loss of blood, and the adrenaline that had overcome me while under attack. I looked down at my forearm. It was healed as well. "You heal me," I said. "Don't stop."

Dimitri's hand tightened on my leg. His fingers moved up my calf, slowly traveled up my thigh, and held my hip. I shuddered around him. His fingers tightened as his pace increased.

Every time his hips rocked, power transferred from him to me. Dimitri reached forward, grabbing my hair and pulling me so that I looked up into the night sky.

Vitality coursed through the connections, pouring into me.

My back arched, taking all he had and offering everything I could. I felt both weakness and strength in that same moment. The duality of it—the exposure, the perfect pain of it—and the outpouring of energy made me scream. Dimitri thrust one last time, his hand tightening in my hair as he followed me over the edge into a pool of fathomless pleasure.

He curled around me, my back pressed against his chest. My heart still pounded as he kissed my ear, my hair, the back of my neck. *I've never felt so alive.*

Power radiated through me, my vision saturated with colors. Sounds traveled to me from great distances. The crackling of the fires miles away, the individual steps and sighs of the zombies wandering the streets below. The blood rushing through my veins.

I rolled, turning to Dimitri. His eyes were gray, lids heavy with exhaustion. *He looks like a man. Not a beast.* I kissed him gently, afraid now that I could hurt him. That I could take too much.

We dressed silently. Dimitri occasionally reached out and brushed against me, his fingers playing with a strand of my hair, lightly caressing my ankle as he tied his shoe.

"Darling, I do not understand what you are." He kissed the top of my head, inhaling my scent. I leaned against his button-down shirt, wrapping my arms around his narrow hips, feeling his hard chest against me. *So strong.* "But in all my centuries on this planet, I've never known this before."

I tilted my head to look up at him. "Known what?"

He held my face and looked at me—his eyes gray blue now, like the ocean at dawn rather than the frozen depths of an iceberg. Dimitri kissed me, his tongue tangling with mine, more of his power drifting to me so that I rose on my tiptoes and pulled him closer. The strength within him intoxicated me.

I broke the kiss and took his hand, walking toward the door that led down into the apartment building.

The door was locked. "Let me." Dimitri reached around me. I stepped aside and saw his forearm strain as he pulled. The door didn't give, and Dimitri's brow furrowed. He glanced at me.

"What's wrong?" I asked.

Dimitri shook his head. "I need to feed." He put both hands on the handle and yanked hard. The metal gave and the door buckled. With one more tug, it opened.

It was dark inside. I reached for the railing. Dimitri wrapped his hand around mine. "Follow me," he said.

The door closed behind us and total darkness descended. I felt his hand on my cheek, his thumb running under my eye, his fingers gliding into my hair. His lips brushed against mine. "I want to drink from you," he said.

I imagined the delicious sinking of his fangs into my flesh, the pleasure of satisfying his hunger, nourishing him.

But I can't. I wasn't sure why, but I felt it in my gut. "I can't let you." My voice came out breathless but strong. His lips skimmed the skin beneath my ear as they traveled down my neck, his tongue flicking against my skin. "I'm sorry Dimitri," I said, "but I can't feed you."

"I understand." He backed away but kept hold of my hand. "You are Megan's." I didn't argue with him. "You can't see in the dark. Shall I carry you?"

"I'm fine, just hold my hand," I answered, feeling strong and steady— I couldn't see the steps, but I could see his energy all around us. I had taken a lot from him.

We started down, and at the first landing, Dimitri opened a door to a hallway. The lights flickered as we walked past apartment doors. "I need to find a human," Dimitri said.

"I thought all the people were moved by the army."

"Not everyone went. Some people are hiding in their apartments."

"How can you tell?"

A smile twitched on his lips. "I can smell them and hear them."

"Hear them?"

"Their blood, moving through their veins." Dimitri's fangs descended slightly. He turned to me. "Yours is singing to me." He made eye contact, and I saw a voracious hunger in his gaze, something that no amount of sex, touch, or feel could heal. He had to suck someone's blood—a life force—to sate it.

Dimitri dropped my hand and kicked a door open. I followed behind him into a living room. A worn couch and two chairs faced a large TV. Small lettering in the upper left-hand corner read "no signal."

Three doors led off the living room, and Dimitri headed toward one of them. A gunshot rang out, the door splintering. Dimitri stumbled back, knocking into me. I fell to the ground and stayed there, covering my head with my hands as more bullets flew.

One ripped through Dimitri's shoulder, and a mist of blood filled the air.

Six bullets and the shooting stopped.

I heard the sound of someone reloading, and Dimitri kicked the door in. I sat up to see a man fall back into the room, Dimitri upon him. The man's scream was cut short as Dimitri dove into his neck.

A woman started screaming. I stood up, feeling her fear grate against my skin, and looked into the bedroom. Dimitri was sucking at the man's neck, the sound strange and vaguely erotic. The man groaned beneath him.

Dimitri is going to kill him.

I turned my attention to the woman—her eyes were wide and she clutched what looked like a doll to her chest. There were no emotions around it, no spark of life. But it wasn't a doll. *It's a child's corpse.* My heart hurt at the realization. "Dimitri," I said. He did not acknowledge me.

I watched from the doorway, my eyes focusing and unfocusing—trying to see that glowing map I'd seen before. There were cords wrapped around both humans—faint lines of light, thin, loose, almost like old-fashioned telephone wires leading off both figures. The man's ran to the woman and back, a crisscross of ties linking them.

Several ran off Dimitri and disappeared through the wall. Others sprung from him and wrapped around the man, pulsing with each suck.

I put my hand on Dimitri's shoulder and ran my fingers up into his hair. "Enough." I pulled him with my mind, twirling lines of my own around him.

The pleasure he was experiencing leaked through the connection. It sent shivers through me. I stepped closer, pressing my body against his. He slowed down. "Do not drain him." My breasts rested on his arm, my emotions tugged against his, attempting to slide between him and his victim.

Dimitri raised his head. The wound on the man's neck was small, just two punctures that oozed blood. Dimitri lapped gently with his tongue and they closed.

He stepped away from the man who wobbled for a moment before dropping to his knees. The man's eyes were glazed, a satisfied smile on his face, like a drunk who's had his fill. His wife whimpered. Her fear was turning Dimitri on. He wanted to feed from her too. I kept my attention on the husband as Dimitri moved toward the wife.

The woman fell silent. The sound of that gentle, erotic slurping started up again. I felt the pleasure they were both experiencing on my back like the sun's beams, a nourishing warmth.

The man's gun was still in his hand. I took it from him. "Where are the extra bullets?" I asked. He did not respond. Looking around, I saw them sitting on a dresser. We were in the couple's bedroom. The child's body was on the ground next to where Dimitri held the woman, his face pressed into her neck.

I put the gun next to the extra bullets. *They will need it.*

I looked down at the child. Skin that was once a deep mahogany now looked pale and gray. It was a girl, must have been about four years old. I didn't see any injuries. *What happened?*

Its eyes opened, and I jumped back. The child had turned. It reached for me, and I stumbled back, knocking into the man. We both tumbled to the ground. The zombie child crawled toward us. I kicked it away, and the man snapped out of his haze.

He stretched toward the child. "Baby," he said, his voice tight with emotion.

"Don't," I said, grabbing for him. But he shrugged me off and reached for his little girl. "No," I said, feeling power pour out of me, the horror of that child biting her father too much for me. Not on top of everything else. I had to stop it.

And I did.

They froze—their fingers centimeters apart. The girl's jaw was open, eyes filmy, a faint green glow behind her irises. Her father's expression loving and pained.

Dimitri's soft suckling continued. I looked over at the bed. The woman laid on her back, Dimitri's head buried in her neck, those ties that disappeared through the wall pulsing.

Fear zinged through me. *What am I doing?* The spell broke, and they moved. I jumped forward, grabbing the girl but holding her away from me. She turned her small face toward mine and snapped the air. Then Dimitri was there. He took the child from me and, turning his back to the rest of the room, crushed the girl's skull. I recognized the sound.

Grief, limitless and impenetrable, expanded, filling the room. The father began to weep, his broad shoulders shuddering. Dimitri threw his influence over the man, but it could not quell the grief that thundered out of him. Dimitri thickened the cloak around the father until he calmed, his eyes going hazy again.

The mother lay motionless on the bed. Dimitri put the little girl's body down gently before bending down and licking the woman's wounds, closing them.

I turned and left the room. Crossing through the living room, I opened another door, hoping to find a bathroom, but discovered a hospital bed. *A child's hospital bed.* I stared at it, the metal sides glimmering in the low light that filtered around me from the living room. Machines surrounded the bed, their lights off.

"I'm sorry," Dimitri said behind me. I closed the door and turned to him. "Blood lust," he said, as if in explanation. "I...it's been a long time since that happened to me." I didn't say anything. "I was very hungry."

"What will happen to them?" I asked.

He looked back at the open door of the bedroom behind him. "They will be taken to our camps, if they survive long enough to be picked up."

"Their little girl," I said, my throat closing as a lump of tears moved up from my gut.

"She died."

"Not from being bitten though," I said. "She was sick." Dimitri didn't say anything. "The dead turn no matter what?" I asked. He nodded. "Will they rise from the ground?" I asked.

"In time," Dimitri said. So calm. So fucking cold. I met his gaze—the gray was gone.

I pushed past him, opening another door that turned out to be the bathroom. I locked myself in and leaned against the wall. Closing my eyes, I took some deep breaths, pulling myself together. *How did I stop them? Where did that power come from, and how can I use it?* I needed to get to the hospital and talk to Dr. Issa Tor.

CHAPTER TWENTY-ONE

I SPLASHED cold water on my face and pulled my hair back into a tight bun again. My eyes were red-rimmed from the tears, but I still looked good. Somehow better than I'd ever looked before. And I felt strong—powerful—and ready for whatever came my way. My mind was solid, unafraid, coming to grips with the trauma all around me. Somehow I was pulling energy from Dimitri. Maybe Dr. Tor would know what the what was going on with me.

When I came out of the bathroom, Dimitri sat on the couch, his hands resting on his knees. His eyes flicked to me. "Are you okay?" he asked.

I nodded. "I need to go to the hospital."

He blurred to my side, his hand around my back, gently pressing me to him, his nose in my hair. Dimitri inhaled, smelling me. "Are you ill?" he asked.

"I need to find Dr. Issa Tor." I pulled the note out of the small pocket of my pants. He stepped back as I unfolded it. I read it over again before handing it to him.

Dear Darling,

I hope that you receive this letter. Please try to call me. Phones will probably be out

soon, but it's worth a try. If you cannot reach me by phone, please try me at the hospital. If the hospital has fallen, go to 67 Adam's Way.
They can help you. Explain that I sent you.

It is vitally important that you reach me, Darling. Try to find me. Use your strength.

I have information about your father, but more importantly, I think that you can save the world.

Dr. Issa Tor

"I know that address," Dimitri said. "67 Adam's Way. It is a warlock society."

"A what?"

He frowned. "You know nothing of witches and warlocks?"

A laugh bubbled up. "You're kidding, right?" Dimitri did not look like he was joking—his lips were firmed into a tight line. "Are they like the stories?" I asked. Because really, what was I supposed to say?

"Depends on the story." Dimitri unleashed a wicked smile. "Are vampires like the stories?"

"Are you afraid of crosses and garlic?"

He didn't answer the question. "This warlock society is one of the oldest. They are record keepers. There is a vast library at 67 Adam's Way. More information about interdimensional beings, the immortal, and the eternal than any other I know of in this world."

"Interdimensional beings, the immortal, and the eternal, huh?" My head spun trying to take all that in. "So they might know what's going on."

"It is clear 'what is going on'," Dimitri said. "The vampire prophecies are coming true. Everything that was predicted is happening."

"What about this?" I pointed at my healed leg—the skin, smooth and flawless under the ripped, blood-encrusted pants. "Not a scratch on me. How is that possible?"

"I don't know," he said, his voice low. "But it does not matter."

"How can the fact that I got bit by a zombie and survived not be of any consequence? I'm immune or something."

"Or something," Dimitri agreed, his voice low. "There is something different about you. Highly intoxicating. I wonder if this warlock has put a spell of some kind over you." He cocked his head, examining me with those pale blue eyes.

I want to make them go gray again.

"If he could create a spell that let humans recover from a zombie bite, why wouldn't he do it to everyone in the world? Why me? I need to go to the hospital and find him," I said, turning toward the door.

Dimitri blurred in front of me, his jaw set. "It is too dangerous."

"Come with me then. Help me."

I saw those strings of light tug at him; they grew taut for a moment before loosening. "What are you looking at?" he asked, his eyes suddenly suspicious.

"Nothing." I brought my gaze to his. "Help me get to the hospital."

He started toward the door. "I'm to bring you back to the house."

I grabbed his hand, stopping him. "Please," I whispered, raising on my tiptoes and kissing his lips softly. "Escort me to the hospital."

His arm wrapped around my waist and one large hand grabbed my ass. *Possessive.* His lips met mine, and I pressed against the hard planes of him. "I will take you," he said, and I wasn't sure what he meant. "Then we will go to the house." *Oh right, to the hospital. He will take me to the hospital. Right.*

He started toward the door but I held his hand, pulling him back for a second. "What will happen to them?" I asked, pointing toward the bedroom.

"Darling." Dimitri cupped my cheek, looking down at me, a hint of gray in the heat of his gaze. "They will die or they will live. Their daughter is gone, and the world as they knew it is over. There is nothing you can do for them."

We'll see about that, I thought as the door closed behind us.

Fires raged to the south and smoke filled the air. I hardly smelled the stench anymore. *I'm getting used to it.*

Flat roofs, all attached, made for a wide and empty highway above the streets. When we reached the end of the block, Dimitri picked me up. I wound my arms around his neck, and he jumped, landing lightly onto the next roof. Wind from his speed pulled my hair from its bun once again.

When he put me down, the hospital was close. There were snipers on surrounding roofs, firing down into a sea of zombies. The bodies below pressed together, all pushing forward, leaning into makeshift barriers of sandbags that surrounded the hospital.

Tanks and Jeeps faced the zombies. Soldiers in fatigues, their rifles firing into the crowd, stood behind the barricade. It was impossible to see their expressions, but the rapid rat-a-tat of the guns made it clear they were not taking much time to think. This was war, and they were trying to win.

However, from our vantage point above the fray, it was clear that the soldiers, the tanks, and the guns were not going to win. Zombies streamed down every street in the direction of the hospital. They came steadily, walking over the bodies of their fallen brethren, unafraid, unarmed, but persistent, deadly, and on the march.

They fought for no philosophy or religion—it was their nature to destroy, to attack and feed on what they'd once been. How could humanity survive such an enemy?

"Take me closer," I said.

"For what?"

"To find Dr. Tor," I said, annoyed.

"It will be overrun soon; there is no reason to risk your life."

"You promised."

Dimitri laughed. "I did no such thing."

I looked down at the melee below. "When will the vampires save these people? When will they destroy them?" I pointed at the zombies beneath us. "What about the camps—when will that be announced?"

"It is done. There is no TV or communications in Crescent City, so civilians don't know, but the army is taking people to them. We can't stop this, Darling. All we can do is save some."

"We have to get to Dr. Tor. I think he can help."

"Those are not my orders. I'm to keep you alive."

I looked up at him. "What does that mean? Can't you help me? Is it possible?"

"Of course it's possible." He gave me a smug smile. "By getting you out of here." He took a step closer, his body thrumming with energy. "Come now."

I narrowed my eyes at him. "I don't follow orders from you." I could see his influence trying to weasel into me. "I'm surprised you'd even try that crap on me after what we've been through together." His eyes widened, and he stopped trying to control me. "Now, take me over there."

He shook his head. "You do not give me orders, human." Those lines flowing off of him, fading into the distance, seemed to glow for a moment. I focused my gaze on his face. "Are you willing to bargain?" he asked.

"Maybe. What do you want?"

"I want you to be mine." His voice was a deep baritone, his smile predatory and hungry.

"I don't even know what that means," I said, annoyed by his request. I was *mine*.

"You must relinquish Megan and choose me." He drew me close, a hand on my lower back.

"Choose you?" I threw up a hand. *Because having sex with you on the roof isn't enough evidence that I'm into you, I guess.*

"Yes," he said, his voice dropping. "And then I could feed from you."

Oh. "I don't think that's a good idea."

Anger flashed in his eyes and thrummed through his aura, making it sparkle silver. "Why not?" he asked.

"I just don't."

"You've fed from me." He pointed to my leg. "Your injuries healed. How is that possible?"

"I don't know. Maybe Dr. Tor can tell us."

"Megan fed from you," he said, his voice cold. "Why not me?"

I looked up at him, holding his gaze. "I'm not letting anyone feed from me anymore," I said.

He laughed, throwing his head back, exposing his elegant throat. "You pretend as if you have a choice."

"You wouldn't—not against my will," I said.

"The only reason I have not taken from you," he said, his voice turning serious, "is because of Megan's claim on you."

"You tried. You asked."

"Yes. If you choose me, I could."

"So, that's my point. You can't unless I choose you."

"Ah," he said with a smile. "But what about Megan? Do you think she will not feed from you?" He pulled me closer and dropped his voice. "She will drain you of every drop."

"She would never hurt me," I said, defiant.

"Megan is not human. She is like me, hungry and cold." He crashed his lips against mine, thrusting his tongue into my mouth. "I will have every part of you," he promised. "I will take you to the hospital and then I will have everything I want from you."

I opened, absorbing his energy. *I will have all of you!*

The snipers did not miss our leap—they fired several shots. Dimitri covered me with his body until we reached the safety of the stairwell leading down to the rest of the hospital. I flew down the steps, taking them two at a time, my hand gliding along the smooth railing.

When we got to the third floor, I peeked through the glass window in the door. Blood was smeared across the wall by the nurses' station. I pushed open the door slowly, listening. *The whir of the computers, buzz of electric lights, my own breath...*

I crossed to the nurse's station, hairs on my arms tingling, Dimitri close behind. Harriet lay on her side, blood pooling around her. A gruesome wound ravaged her neck and one shoulder.

The TV was knocked off its perch; the screen cracked and blackened —the wiring inside fried when it hit the ground. Files were spilled around the small space behind the counter. Harriet's chair was turned over. *She fought but it didn't do her any good.*

My fingers gripped the end of the counter, eyes riveted to her still form. She wasn't seizing or moving. But she would start soon. I walked around to crouch by her side. I'd never been back there before, never had a reason until today. "We need to find a way to restrain her," I said to Dimitri, "so that when she wakes up she won't hurt anyone."

Dimitri bent down beside her and placed his hand on her head. "No!" I yelled. "Don't kill her."

He looked up at me. "She is already dead."

"But if I'm immune then maybe we can come up with a vaccine."

Dimitri shook his head. "There is no vaccine for bleeding out, Darling." Then with what looked like no pressure at all, he crushed her skull, her brains squirting out like a ketchup packet. I gasped and turned away, covering my eyes. "It is for the best," Dimitri said to my back. I nodded, swiping at the tears sneaking out of my eyes. *How much more of this can I take?*

"Let's find Issa." I didn't look at her again—blocking the memory of the nurse I knew, the living, breathing woman. *She is gone.* There was nothing I could do for her. I had to stay focused on what I *could* accomplish.

We went back out into the waiting room, and I led Dimitri toward the door to the exam rooms. Dimitri grabbed my bicep and held me back. "Wait," he said, a small smile on his lips. "Let me go first, the immortal vampire who can kill zombies, instead of the woman who was almost killed by zombies less than two hours ago."

"Making jokes?" I asked, annoyed but at the same time grateful he was with me, worrying about me, helping me survive. I might be immune to zombie bites, but doubted I'd survive bleeding out like Harriet. *Don't think about it.*

"Do not worry," Dimitri said, his voice turning serious. "I will not allow you to be hurt in any way." He stared down at me, his eyes boring into mine.

"Thank you," I said, not breaking eye contact. Dimitri shook his head slowly. "What?"

"I do not know," he said. "And that is...uncomfortable."

"Welcome to my world," I said with a hiccup of a laugh that verged on a sob. "Let's find Dr. Tor so we can get some answers."

"Stay here." Dimitri blurred through the doors, leaving them swinging on their hinges. I listened intently for that strange strangled sound the zombies made. It was so pained I almost had sympathy for the death-hungry creatures. Were they so different from us? Weren't we all driven by our natures? Did any of us really have free will?

I heard slamming and banging, a sickening skull-cracking sound that was becoming far too familiar. Standing in the waiting room, staring at the cracked TV, the overturned chairs, the smears of blood, I shook slightly, terrified by the absolutely overwhelming hordes of them.

Standing there alone, my faith that I could help faltered. *What can I possibly do against this disaster?*

Dimitri pushed open the door and motioned for me to come with him. "I checked the rooms," he said as I followed him.

How long ago did I follow Dr. Tor down this same hall, with its watercolors of peaceful landscapes? The paintings were askew now—some knocked off the wall altogether. Broken glass crunched under our shoes.

"I didn't find anyone living," Dimitri said. "Perhaps your Dr. Issa is dead."

I peered into the open doors: empty, empty, zombie sprawled across exam table, goopy blood dripping slowly from its crushed skull, brains splattered across the wall. The smell was sickening, and I swallowed bile. It wasn't Dr. Tor.

There was no spark of life anywhere. Just death. "He's probably down in the ER," I said, turning back toward the exit.

Dimitri grabbed my arm again. "I go first, remember?" he said. "That is the only way I'll do this with you."

"Okay," I said, "but let's hurry."

He smiled, a twinkle coming into his eye. "In that case I should carry you."

"I'll walk," I said. "I'm not totally helpless."

"No," he agreed. "Just slow."

Whatever.

We crossed back through the waiting room and into the stairwell. As we approached the ground floor, we heard shouting, rapid gunshots, and feet running. People began streaming up toward us.

Men and women, some in plain clothes, others in scrubs, were sprinting up the stairs, their eyes wild with panic. Dimitri pulled me to the side and we slunk down the wall, people bumping against us. A woman, holding a baby in her arms, tripped up the steps. Dimitri caught her arm, steadying her. She yanked free, running for her life.

"Where are they going?" I asked as I watched her disappear into the crowd.

"Away from them," Dimitri answered. "We should, too."

"Not until I find Issa," I said, pushing him forward.

The gunshots grew louder, the crowd more frantic, the closer we got to the first floor and emergency room. Then there were soldiers coming up, facing backward, their guns aimed down.

One elbowed me as he backed up the stairs, knocking me into Dimitri. "Get back!" he yelled as I fell into Dimitri's arms. The soldier looked over his shoulder, up at Dimitri, and his jaw went slack.

Dimitri glared down at him, upset by the soldier's rough treatment of me. The crowd quieted then parted for us as Dimitri's influence filled the stairwell, pressing into all the minds of the humans, controlling their thoughts and actions.

He took my hand, keeping me close to his side. The soldiers raised their weapons as we passed, as though it was some sort of processional.

When we reached the first floor, it was all soldiers wearing army fatigues meant for the desert; the sandy shades almost fit in with the scuffed white walls of the hospital stairwell, but not quite. Several men leaned against the door. Zombies pressed on the window.

A gunshot on the far side exploded one of the zombie's faces, painting the glass with blood. Three more gunshots, then another two, followed by a knock at the door. "We're alive, let us in!" came a voice I thought was Issa's. The soldiers exchanged looks.

"I think that's him," I said, holding onto Dimitri's forearm with one hand, my fingers linked with his—the vampire's influence a welcome balm.

Dimitri nodded his head, and the three soldiers on the door stepped back. The overwhelming smell of blood filled the narrow stairwell. Issa and Basil fell through the opening, both of them spattered with blood and guts.

Basil slammed the door and the three soldiers returned to their post. "We've lost the front of the building," he said, stating the obvious. The soldier looked at him with glassy eyes.

Issa turned and spotted me. "Darling!" he yelled. "My God." He stepped forward as if to touch me and then, looking down at his gore-covered scrubs, stopped. "You're alive," he said, tears welling in his eyes.

"Yes," I said, letting go of Dimitri to take Issa's hand, wanting to make sure he was really there, that I'd found him. His skin was sticky with blood. *He is so brave.* Dr. Issa Tor risked his life to help people. That's the kind of human I wanted to be. "Come with me," he said, pushing up the stairs, our fingers still linked.

Dimitri's hand landed on Issa's shoulder. "Let go of her," he said, his eyes flashing gray, jealous and angry—almost human in their emotion.

Issa raised his eyebrows as he looked at the vampire. They were about the same height, but that is where any resemblance ended. Dimitri's shoulders were broad, skin and hair pale, suit elegant...gaze deadly. Issa's narrow frame spoke of a wiry strength, his intelligent eyes sparked with life and purpose—he wasn't a killer. *Issa Tor saves lives and Dimitri takes them...*

"I want her to be safe, too," he told the vampire. *So they have that in common.*

Dimitri growled. "Do not touch her."

"That's up to her," Issa said, his voice quiet...brave.

"It's fine," I told Dimitri then squeezed Issa's hand. "Let's go," I said, pushing up the stairs. We passed the soldiers and the frightened staff back up to the third floor. Issa led the way through the waiting room and down the hall to his office.

Basil and Dimitri followed us. "Can we have some privacy?" I asked. Neither man moved. Issa nodded at Basil, who looked up at Dimitri. "Please," I said to him.

His eyes flashed gray and he turned to Issa. "Do not harm her. Do not—" He pursed his lips but did not continue. Dimitri grunted in frustration before following Basil out of the room. I turned to Tor.

"Now tell me, how can I save the world?"

CHAPTER TWENTY-TWO

Issa's eyes ran over my body, stopping at the knives on my hips and chain around my waist. "Are you hurt?" he asked.

"I'm fine," I said. "Better than fine." He made eye contact and then turned away, nodding. "Are you all right?" I asked. "You're covered in blood."

"It's not mine," he said, looking down at himself.

"Is it infected?"

"Some," he answered. "I better change."

I turned my back as he pulled off his shirt. I heard him rustling around in a cabinet, and when I peeked back, he was slipping on a clean shirt. His chest was smooth and hard. The doctor had a six pack, and a trail of dark hair running down the center of it.

I turned my gaze away again as he began to pull off his pants, feeling that hunger crawl up my throat. I bit inside my cheek, pulling my focus to the pain, ignoring the urges inside of me.

"I want you to tell me who you are," I said, not turning around. "Who you really are. Dimitri says that the address you gave me is a warlock society."

"Yes," Issa said, his voice soft. "I guess you've learned a lot since I saw you last. Traveling with vampires. Basil told me your red-headed friend saved us."

"Yes, she did," I answered, turning around. He was dressed in a fresh pair of aqua green scrubs and was using an antibacterial wipe to clean his face and neck. "There is something wrong with her, though."

"What do you mean?" he asked, tossing the towelette into the trash. He opened a drawer in his desk and pulled out a string of black beads.

"Her transformation was not complete. She still has one green eye," I said as Issa crossed in front of me toward the door.

He stopped at my words, turning to me, his dark brows arched. "Really?" he said. "That is very unusual."

I coughed another one of those laugh sobs. "That's the unusual thing?"

He smiled shyly, almost embarrassed. Issa turned away from me and, facing the door, raised the beads and muttered under his breath for a moment.

"What are you doing?" I asked.

He did not answer. A power floated out of the beads, like smoke. It glowed yellow, seeming to be lit from within, and crept into the creases of the door, building some kind of barrier.

Issa lowered the beads and the smoke stayed in place. "So that your vampire friend can't hear or smell us," he said.

"You're a witch, a warlock...that's a spell?"

Gunfire, close and loud, made me jump. "We don't have much time." He started back to his desk.

"You need to tell me what you know about me," I said, grabbing his arm and stopping him.

"What do you mean?"

"Don't play with me, Issa," I said, my voice venomous, angrier than I expected. "You knew when I kissed you—you knew what I was."

"And what are you?" he asked, looking down at me, his voice almost breathless. Our bodies close, my hand on his arm tingling with current.

"I don't know." My voice cracked—the doubts and fears swirling in my mind trying to escape. I forced myself to step away from him. It was hard. I wanted to grab him, kiss him, suck the energy from between his lips. "Am I a monster? Like a vampire or something?"

"What happened? Did you...with that vampire?"

"His name is Dimitri, and he saved my life," I said. "I was bit. Multiple times."

"You were?" He looked me up and down, saw the ripped leg of my pants and dropped to his knees, reaching for me.

I stepped out of his grasp. "You shouldn't touch me," I warned.

"I can take it," he said, not looking up at me. His dark hair was mussed, out of control, and that lack of perfection, the flaws of him, that was what I craved—the humanity inside of him. I could see it. *I crave his weakness.*

"You're human," I said.

"Yes," he answered, reaching for my leg again.

I let him touch me. His fingers pushed the cloth away gently, revealing the smooth skin below. Not even a scratch where that zombie took a chunk out of me.

As I looked down at him, I unfocused my eyes, searching for Issa's power—his spark. A weakness at the center of him granted him some kind of power. Some kind of connection to the natural world that Dimitri did not have... that I did not share, either. *Mortality?*

"You're not a regular human, though," I said as his fingers explored my calf.

"I'm a warlock. My family has been practicing for centuries."

"But you can die. A zombie bite would kill you?"

"Yes."

"What can I do to stop it?" I asked. "You said I could save the world."

"You're immune." He stood, his body close to mine now. "And I think that means we could use your blood to find a cure."

"What do you need?"

He crossed to a cabinet behind his desk. "I need to take some blood from you. Run tests, see what kind of antibodies you have."

"It was after I had sex with Dimitri," I told Issa, his back still turned to me. He stopped shuffling in the cabinet and faced me. "I was bitten, he saved me, and then we...on a roof, and I felt myself healing. I knew what was happening. I was feeding from him."

Issa nodded. "Yes, and you fed from me."

"What about Megan? Did I feed from her? Is that why she got sick?" I asked, my voice catching again.

"I don't know, Darling. I've never met one of your kind before."

"My kind? What am I?"

"I'm not totally sure."

"What does that mean?" My voice rose with anger and frustration.

"If you are what I suspect, then you are very rare." He approached me, a needle and several vials in his hand. "There are stories, but…"

I shook my head, trying to clear it. "Tell me what you know about me, about my father?"

"He was a warlock."

"From your society?"

"No." Issa motioned for my arm, and I held it out. He tied a tourniquet around my bicep. His fingers brushed against my skin, and heat rose in my cheeks, that hunger burning in my gut. "He was very powerful. Perhaps the most powerful warlock in all the worlds."

"All the worlds?"

Issa slid the needle into my skin.

A lock of pitch black hair fell over his forehead as he focused on my arm. He removed the tourniquet with a snap, and my blood flowed through the needle.

"Darling." His gaze rose to meet mine, and I turned away. *If I look at him, I'll steal from him.* "There are as many worlds as possibilities."

"I don't understand."

"Few do," he said. "The most brilliant humans in all the universe don't understand. There are an infinite amount of universes—each unique and yet many similar. Your father, he learned to pass between them."

My mind tripped over itself. *An infinite amount of dimensions.* "He traveled between them? How?"

"I don't know," Issa said. He replaced the vial attached to the needle.

"How much are you taking?" I asked.

"As much as I can."

"I will need to feed after." The hunger inside me stirred—like a beast who, now that I'd unchained it, demanded more with each breath.

"It would be my honor," Issa whispered. He was staring at me.

"I can kill you." My gaze fell to his lips—soft and so very human.

"I know."

I jerked my attention away. "What about my mother, who was she?"

"She was like you. Very rare. There is very little science, only myth about her, about you."

"What is the myth?"

"A descendant of Lilith, the first human woman ever made, expelled from the Garden of Eden for refusing to lie under Adam. Banished to the earth, to wander alone. She is considered a demon by many—said to steal the seed of men as they sleep…steal their life force." He looked down at my arm and replaced the vial again. Three vials now waited, filled with my blood. "But that is just a myth, Darling. Women are always demonized in stories. Who knows where you really came from, how your kind came to exist."

"I can steal your life force though." I said it quietly. Issa didn't respond. "Why do you think I'm immune?" He shifted, uncomfortable with the question. "What?"

Issa sighed. "I don't know—but the myth says that part of Lilith's punishment is that she could not have children. So she stole children and made them her own…demon children. Zombies."

"But she had me."

Issa nodded. "Yes, exactly. It's just a story. But…it is thought that your kind cannot survive childbirth. There can be only one of you alive at a time." He put a full vial on his desk and placed another one on the needle. It began to fill, and I turned away again, staring at the closed door, the yellow smoke thick in its crevices. "Your father took you to an almost uninhabited dimension, hoping to keep you safe until you matured."

"He was killed," I said. "By wolves."

"He tried to send you to my society." I looked back at him. He met my gaze. "But we missed you. He sent you through the portal, and we thought you'd come out here but you ended up much further north."

"What do you mean? He sent me to your society. You missed me?" I pulled away from him but he followed, the needle staying in my arm, the blood continuing to flow.

"We have been searching for you. When I saw the markers on your bone marrow in the database, I thought it might be you. I came searching for you."

"Why didn't you just tell me? Why all this sneaking around?"

"I had to be sure." He removed the filled vial, replacing it with another. "You don't understand, Darling—your father was the first mortal to ever learn to manipulate the dimensional passageways."

"Who can then? Vampires?"

"No, only gods and their descendants…and your kind."

"Gods!" I yelled. "There are gods?"

Issa removed the last vial and put a cotton swab over the needle as he removed it. "Yes," he answered. "There are gods."

Vampires, zombies, and now gods.

I was the descendant of a demon maker. My father was a warlock with knowledge beyond any others. Though, obviously he wasn't *that* good since I got lost…

I couldn't think; my brain was stuttering with information, and there was nowhere for me to turn. And then my lips were on Issa's. His were warm and accepting. I pushed him up against the desk, my fingers lacing into his hair, holding him tight to me.

Hands roamed up and down my back, one tangled in my hair. He moaned against my lips as I felt that energy source inside of him. That flawed yet powerful center gave itself to me, rushing out of him, filling me with its strength and easing my hunger…calming my mind.

Gunshots in the hall broke through the haze of my lust and I pulled away, looking toward the door, my vision vibrating.

The door burst open. Dimitri—eyes fiery blue—grabbed me around the waist and yanked me from between Issa's legs. I fell back, stumbling and almost falling to the ground. Basil caught me. Dimitri went to grab Issa, but Dr. Tor put up his hand, spoke quickly in a foreign tongue, and Dimitri fell away, holding the sides of his head and moaning in pain.

"What are you doing?" I yelled, pushing free of Basil and hurrying to Dimitri's side.

"He was in a blood lust, was going to kill me," Issa said, his voice sounding weak. "I stopped him." He leaned against the desk, his skin gray and eyes sunken.

"Stop," I said. "Please, you're hurting him."

Issa dropped his hand, as though it was too heavy to hold up anyway.

"Sir," Basil said, "we must go. The hospital has been fully breached."

Dimitri turned to me, his face back to that porcelain mask—his eyes ice blue again. *I'm starting to hate that color.* "Your time is up," he said to me. "I will take you back now." Cords stretched away from him, tight with tension and pulsing. *They pull at him, control him.*

"Come with me to my society," Issa said. "You can learn more there.

We have all the records. More information about your father. There are labs there. We can work together to find a cure. You'll be safe."

I looked from him to Dimitri. "I have to go with him," I said to the vampire. "I have to find out what I am."

"I must take you back to Brad." The cords vibrated. *Can I snap them?*

"I'll let you feed from me," I said.

His expression shifted, his eyes flashing gray, but then the cords glowed brightly and his gaze shuttered. "Think about it," I said, stepping closer to Dimitri, pushing my hair back from my neck. "Don't you want to taste me?"

"Yes." He licked his lips, pupils growing.

"We'll just go to the society first, and then we'll go back to Megan. I promise. Just a couple of hours." I put my hand on his chest. He covered it with his, lips softening into an amused smile. *The vampire can find humor anywhere.* "I won't abandon Megan, Dimitri, but I have to find out what is going on. If I can really help."

"We will escort you," Issa offered.

Dimitri looked over my head at him. "We do not need your help," he snarled—the amusement turning to disdain in a flash.

"We must go," Basil said again, even more urgently.

Dimitri picked me up and threw me over his shoulder. My surroundings blurred. Then we were on the roof, back out into the night. Dimitri took a running leap, and with my head hanging down, I saw the legions of zombies flowing over the sandbags and into the open doors of the hospital below.

CHAPTER TWENTY-THREE

DIMITRI PUT me down once we reached the warlock society. I'd never gone down Adam's Way before, despite it being in the center of town and not far from my apartment or the clubs where Megan and I played. The building at number 67 was surrounded by a high stone wall, the top of it six feet above my head. "I've never noticed this place before," I said to Dimitri. "Isn't that weird?"

"No, they hide it," Dimitri answered.

"How?" I asked, looking over at him. His hair shone under the street lamps, the elegant cut of his suit catching the light in sharp lines. My breath caught as I stared at him—gorgeous as a statue, fierce and loyal— how did I get here?

"They use a cloaking spell," Dimitri said, looking over at me and cocking his head at my expression.

I cleared my throat, pulling myself together. "Sure," I said with a shrug. "A cloaking spell, why not?"

The decorative pattern on the iron gates swirled so thick I couldn't see through it. I ran my fingers along the grooves as Dimitri rang the bell. A small red light glowed on the panel next to a lens. *They can see us.*

"How may we help you?" came a voice through the speaker.

"Issa Tor sent us," Dimitri said, leaning slightly toward the speaker box.

"One moment," the voice responded.

A zombie stumbled around the corner, followed closely by another. Spotting us in the center of the block, they picked up their pace.

"Wait here." Dimitri blurred down the street. His form solidified in front of the zombies. One fell and then the other, their skulls pierced by a blade that shone in Dimitri's hand—he bent down to wipe it off on one of the zombie's jackets. *Sure, that makes sense. Need to keep your weapons clean.*

My vision fogged. The street distorted. Tingles started at the top of my head and crawled down my body. *Now I'm having a seizure? Great.* I closed my eyes as a wave of nausea racked through me.

When it passed, I opened my eyes—I was standing in a formal garden surrounding a large and grand building, made of stone, with a central tower and large ornate columns. *I'm inside the warlock compound.* The front door opened, and a man wearing a blood red robe, tied at the waist with a thick rope, hurried down the steps toward me.

"Darling!" I heard Dimitri yell, his voice faint.

"I'm in here," I yelled, turning back to the gate. "Dimitri, can you hear me?"

"Darling! Darling!" he yelled again, his voice holding a desperate edge that sounded almost like fear.

The robed figure approached me quickly, his feet making hardly any sound on the paved paths. "Come," he said, motioning with his arm. "We must go inside."

"No." I backed up toward the gate. He grabbed my arm. "Let go of me!" I struggled against his tight grasp.

"Please," he said, his eyes wide with worry. "Don't touch the gate."

"Why?" I said looking at it.

"We must not let him in. Dimitri is very dangerous."

"Not to me, he's not. You on the other hand..." I looked down at where he held me to make my point.

His hazel eyes, magnified by his thick glasses, blinked rapidly. "Oh," he said. "No, no, I wouldn't. I couldn't hurt you."

"Then let go of me."

He glanced around the garden as if searching for help. "But"—he bit his lip—"you can't let the vampire in."

"I'm not staying without him."

A form began to materialize between me and the gate. Faint sparkles solidified into a man hunched down into his robes, as if gravity had a personal stake in pushing him into the ground. However, his sharp eyes made it clear that it'd take more than a law of nature to get him down.

The old man reached out and took my arm lightly—his hand gnarled and spotted with age. That strange sensation passed through me again, and I closed my eyes against the twisting world.

When the nausea passed and I opened my eyes, we were standing in a library the length of a football field. Wooden ladders ran on metal tracks, allowing access to the highest shelves. Large tables were dotted around the center of the space, green lamps illuminating their glossy surfaces.

"Where are we?" I asked.

"Not to worry." He released my arm. His voice did not have the normal wavering of age I associated with men of his advanced years. "We are inside the building. Your vampire lover is not far. We will reunite you soon." He stepped over to a table covered in books.

"Why should I trust you?" I asked as he pulled one of the leather-bound manuscripts toward him.

He looked up at me, his brown eyes flashing in the warm light of the library. "Your father did."

I jutted my chin up, instantly wary. "Why should I believe you?"

He opened the book and removed a folded sheet of vellum paper. I could see black lettering though the thin paper. He handed it to me. "You must recognize his handwriting."

I took the sheet from him, not taking my eyes off his—they did not glaze as I expected. His lip twitched in a smile. "I have protected myself with a powerful spell that few know and even fewer believe works. If you were more powerful, it would not."

"Protecting you from what, exactly?"

His brow knitted and worry rippled through his gaze. "I have so much to teach you, but first, please, read the note."

I unfolded it gently, the paper's texture familiar. My father wrote letters weekly. He'd promised that someday he would tell me about them but…that day never came.

My breath caught as I looked down at his neat handwriting—written with the feather quill pens he let me help make.

Father used the feathers from the turkeys that we hunted. He'd choose the three longest from each wing. When I was very young, he let me remove the ribbing from the bottom portion, enough so that his hand fit comfortably. By the time I was seven and my hand steadier, he let me use the small knife to finish them.

"Cut the edge at an angle," he'd said, leaning over me, his breath on my hair.

My bottom lip between my teeth, I sliced the end of the feather at forty-five degrees.

"Perfect, Darling." There was a smile in his voice. "Now trim the end flat." I repositioned the feather, laying the longer edge down, then cut off the sharp tip. "Nicely done, now what?"

"Create the path for the ink."

"Yes, Darling, that's right. You'll be making all my pens for me soon," he said with a laugh. I almost heard the sound as I looked down at the letter addressed to me.

My Dearest Daughter,

If you are reading this, I am gone, and we did not have the time I hoped for together. As I write this you are by the fire, working on your math lessons. A strong and precocious girl of eight. My heart aches that you may someday have to read this letter—that we will be apart.

But do not be afraid, my Darling, for you are stronger than you know. Stronger even than your mother.

This correspondence is in possession of my oldest friend, Tyronios Templer. Listen to him, he can be trusted. Tyronios and his fellow warlocks have more knowledge about you and your kind than any other order I have come across in all the worlds. They will protect you until you grow into the powerful woman I know you will be.

Listen to Tyronios and learn from him. The Universe may depend upon you someday, my dearest darling daughter.

Forever,

Your loving Father,
Darconia Price III

A tear fell onto the thin paper, the ink under it blurring and distorting. I swiped at my face and looked up at Tyronios. "Aren't you a little late?" I asked. "I'm already a woman."

"I apologize." Sadness flashed in his bright eyes. "We expected you to arrive here. But dimensional travel is always complicated and unpredictable."

A tear slipped down my cheek. "What do you want from me?"

"It is not what I want from you, Darling, but what I am offering." He swept his arm toward the table of books. "This is everything we know of your kind."

"And what kind is that? What do you mean? " I heard myself yelling, the paper in my hand crumpled as my fingers curled into an angry fist—the beast inside me stirring.

The older warlock stayed calm, his eyes steady and voice even. "There are lots of names for your kind. Succubus, Daughter of Lilith, Dream Stealer, Heart Beater, Goddess, Queen. There is no end of names that the worlds create. Every one of them true somewhere, and all of them false in other places. But you, Darling, are now responsible for the next chapter."

He opened one of the books, flipping through the pages until he found what he wanted. "Come, look." He waved me forward.

I stepped closer, peering over his shoulder. Tyronios pointed at an illustration. At the center, a beautiful woman with long dark hair like mine stood at the center of a battlefield. She held a long staff; it penetrated the head of a victim at her feet. In the scene around her, figures pulled off heads, thrust swords through midsections, bit each other. It was bloody, horrible chaos in black and white, except for one bit of color—the woman's eyes: they were the same green as mine.

"Helen. She lived 10,000 years ago. Ruled an army of vampires a million strong. Conquered seventy worlds before reaching full maturity and giving birth to her daughter, Stella." Tyronios turned through the pages, stopping at another lithograph. This woman sat in a tree, surrounded by birds and animals that watched her with adoration. Same black hair and green eyes but a totally different woman—her expression was one of love and compassion, not cruelty and power. "Stella was the product of Helen and a woodsman she attacked, not realizing he was a warlock. Helen's pregnancy was unexpected, and when she died, her vampires expired with her, leaving Stella alone in the woods. She was raised by foxes." He pointed to a small grouping of foxes at the bottom of the illustration. "She never left her world."

"How many?" I asked. "How many before me?"

Tyronios looked up at me. "At least fifteen," he said. "But there is no way to be sure."

"How do you know any of this is true?" I asked. "If it all happened so long ago?"

Tyronios pulled over another book. "We cross-reference," he said. "We have books from many different dimensions, and if we find references that match in more than one, we think of it as possible. More than ten, we think of it as likely. More than twenty," he smiled, "true enough to trust."

"So I can travel between the dimensions?" I asked.

"You should be able to. I don't know how, though."

"What about vampires?"

"Not without help. Most of the ones in this world don't believe in multiple dimensions. They are small-minded, deeply religious, and dedicated to an ancient text that does not deal with the entirety of the universe."

"But they predicted the zombie apocalypse," I said.

Tyronios shrugged and smiled. "They believe in their own deities. One who will die for the sins of the undead."

"The undead? Does that include zombies and vampires?"

"Yes, in some worlds they also count ghosts and disembodied spirits."

"They think someone is going to die for their sins. I don't understand."

"The question of the soul, what happens to the soul of the undead, is debated in every world in the universe."

I raised my eyebrows. "Is it clear what happens to the soul of the just plain dead?"

Tyronios smiled and shook his head. "I suppose not. In this world, in the religion of most vampires, called Emmulisivity, it is believed that the son of a powerful God lives in this world, dying and being reborn, waiting for the rise of the zombies, so that he may be bitten and rise again. By sacrificing his own child, this God purges all of the undead of their sins and they inherit the earth, keeping all humans under their control, for their own pleasure and nourishment."

"What do you think? Do you think this savior is real, the prophecy?"

"We believe the 'savior'"—Tyronios made air quotes and his voice dripped with condescension—"is an egomaniac, a very ancient being, related to a God but not his direct son. He travels from world to world, following the scent of the zombies, dying by their hand and rising for his own ego. We do not believe the souls of the undead are saved by him. He enjoys the worship of the vampire. Some in our society even believe that he helps to spread zombism between the worlds for his own satisfaction."

"Wow," I said. "So you believe that he exists?"

"Yes, we are hunting him, in fact."

"You think he is here, in our world?"

Tyronios nodded. "Yes, but he will move on soon."

I picked up a book and flipped through the pages. Illustrations of dark-haired women in the throes of passion filled the pages. I stopped on one. The woman was between two men, one in front and one behind. She arched between them, her long hair streaming down her bare back. The woman's eyes were open, rays of green light burning out of them toward the top of the page. "Considered to be the best way for your kind to gain power," Tyronios said.

I closed the book, my cheeks hot, hunger clawing at me, the images in the book sparking that rapacious need.

"What does this have to do with now? With the plague that is destroying this city? Why do you and Issa and my father think that I can stop it?"

"Issa thinks your blood holds a cure. Your father believed your powers could stop the spread of the disease. I believe that Lilith, the first of your kind, started it. And you can end it."

"Go on."

"Lilith would not be subservient to Adam," Tyronios explained. "Some legends say she left and others claim she was expelled. However, Lilith did not wander the earth alone, as Adam and God hoped. She met the archangel Samil, who coupled with her for centuries. In some worlds they are portrayed as evil—death bringers, harborers of doom, creators of the zombie apocalypse. In others they are remembered as freedom fighters, champions of equality, and two souls that loved as one."

"And you think of them as the zombie makers?" I asked.

"You are immune, Darling, are you not?"

"So are vampires," I said.

"But only because they are already dead."

"Whereas I'm alive."

"According to the rhythm of your heart."

I raised my eyebrows. "Is that what makes you alive?"

"Vampire and zombie hearts do not beat."

"Don't they?" I asked, thinking of Dimitri's heart. I had felt it beat along with mine.

Tyronios cocked his head. "Have you heard one beat?"

"When I was with Dimitri…I felt his heart beat." He turned to the books. "What about Megan? She is only half turned."

"Half turned?" he looked up at me. "That is very rare."

"That's what Issa said. I think she is still capable of love."

Tyronios shook his head. "Vampires cannot love. They can obsess, but it is not the same as love." His finger scanned down a page and then he flipped through the book. "There is one reference." He traced the words with his finger. "One world that believes Samil was a vampire. The first vampire. And that Lilith turned him into an angel. Brought him back to life. Eternal life."

I leaned over him, but the book was in a language I didn't recognize. Shaking my head, I stepped back. Tyronios continued to read. A pull in my gut made me startle. *Megan is in trouble.* How did I know that?

"What is it?" Tyronios asked.

"Issa has my blood," I said. "I need to go now."

"But you have only just arrived. Don't you want to learn about yourself?" He left the book open and stepped toward me.

I glanced at the pile of manuscripts. "There is nothing about me in those books," I said. "That is the past."

Tyronios shook his head. "But, Darling, how can you say that?"

"Every one of us is different. Maybe we all get power from sex, but we all wield it differently. If my immunity is replicable, then you will discover that in your labs, not in your library."

"But it may be in a spell, Darling. We can work together to end this plague. You are right that these books cannot tell you about yourself, but they are your history. And history cannot be ignored—especially when it keeps repeating."

A crash from the hall drew our attention to the doors. Tyronios rushed past me and locked them. "That vampire has breached our borders. He must be very old."

"I was just leaving anyway."

"But what about the letter from your father? Don't you see you need us?"

I stared down at the older man. "I needed you when I was a child," I spat at him, angry with all that could have been. If they'd found me instead of those police officers, if I'd been raised in this library instead of in the home of a monster, how different would my life have been? Then I felt the pull from Megan again and remembered that without the mistakes made, I never would have met her. And I didn't want to be without Megan, no matter what any book said about her ability to love, the location of her soul, or anything else. "Now what I need is to go and get my friend."

"It is so dangerous," Tyronios said. "We can train you, help develop your gifts, and then you can save her. It will be so much easier."

I was tempted by his offer but knew that the world would not wait for me to gain strength. If I wanted to free Megan from her parent's grasp, now was the time to do it. "I have to go," I said.

"We need you here," he pleaded. "Together we can stop this plague."

The door to the library burst open, and Dimitri, his shirt blood-spattered and face contorted in rage, stormed in. He blurred to me, his arms wrapping around me, and we smashed into the table full of books. His hands touched me everywhere—as if making sure I was real. "Don't leave me," he said against my ear, his voice so low only I could hear.

"I'm here," I whispered against his hair. Tyronios watched us from by the door, his eyes wide with shock. He ran to the books and flipped through pages. Dimitri kissed my neck, whispering my name. Power coursed through my veins, pulling from his lips, his wet hungry tongue.

Tyronios read the words under his breath and then looked back up at us. "A vampire in love," he said. "Has he drunk from you?" I shook my head. "I never thought it was possible."

I pushed lightly on Dimitri's shoulders, and he eased off of me but held his arm around my waist, keeping me close. "I want this to end as much as you. As much as any being capable of feeling compassion. It is horrible. But now I need to get to Megan. I can feel that she needs me. I will come back if I can. But first, I've got some vampires to deal with."

CHAPTER TWENTY-FOUR

BEFORE WE RETURNED to Megan's parents' house, I needed all the strength I could get. I didn't know how to free Megan, but I *knew* that I could…somehow. That core of strength inside of me could do anything.

We left the mansion at 67 Adam's Way—the warlocks didn't even try to stop us. They just watched Dimitri pick me up and carry me out. He took a running leap over the high stone wall, and we landed on the quiet street. "I want a shower and a change of clothes," I told him.

Dimitri nodded. I tried to climb out of his arms but he held me tight. "Hey." I placed a hand on his chest, and he looked down at me. "It's okay," I promised.

Dimitri licked his lips, his eyes dark in the low light. "You are so young and have seen so little." A subtle smile pulled at his lips. "And yet you try to comfort me." He gave his head a small shake. "You have changed me, Darling. And I don't understand it."

"Me either. But I know I can walk." I smiled at him.

He put me down slowly, keeping a hand on my lower back. We didn't go far, only about two blocks, to where there were apartment buildings. Dimitri broke down the front door and we entered one of the ground floor spaces.

He picked up a couch, lifting it as though it was made of cardboard, and blocked our entrance, offering a small protection from zombies—it would slow them down at least.

Dimitri took my hand and led me through the dark.

His energy pulsed as we entered a bathroom—I felt tile under my feet and sensed the small space as Dimitri's influence tightened around us to fit.

He leaned forward, and I heard a shower start, the spray a welcome sound. I was filthy.

"There is no hot water," Dimitri said. His fingers ran under my shirt, brushing my bare abdomen and pulling it over my head. He left a trail of kisses as he bent down to remove my pants and shoes. His own clothing rustled as he removed it.

Holding my waist, Dimitri moved me closer to the spray. "I will make you warm." Heat came off him, and power flowed over my body, heating me as the water hit.

I leaned my head back, the blood and grime washing away. "We don't have much time," Dimitri said. "The sun will be up soon."

"You can't be in the sun?" I asked. Dimitri reached behind me and brought a bar of soap to my belly.

"Not for long," he answered, his lips close to my shoulder. "I must feed from you." His tongue found my pulse, bringing more heat up against my skin.

"Where is the shampoo?" I asked. He squeezed some in my hand, and I began to wash my hair as he continued to clean my body. His strong and knowledgeable hands glided over me as if they always had—as if we'd always been together.

Who knew what we were to each other—all I was certain of in that moment, with him so close, keeping me warm, cleaning me, was that love pulsed between us. A connection that fed me—that I'd have died without.

Is he the man from my dream? I don't know.

The room was pure darkness except for the glow of him...*of his what?* Was it a soul? The glowing cloud of Dimitri contrasted with the tight red center of me. I looked down at myself, invisible in the darkness except for the diamond of color pulsing.

I reached up to touch his face, and he leaned down, his lips finding mine. We kissed slowly, luxuriously, as if the world was not coming apart at the seams, as if the sun was not about to rise, as if time was nothing to us.

I took the soap from him and washed his body, tracing along the smooth planes and hard angles of his beautiful form. He sucked in air when I touched between his legs. I wrapped my hand around him before dropping to my knees.

The water sprayed down my back as I explored him with my mouth. His hands tightened in my wet hair as I sucked him in. "Darling," he whispered, the sound loud and echoing in the small bathroom. "Please," he begged. "Say you are mine."

I released him and stood again. He picked me up, wrapping my legs around his hips. Dimitri's strong hands held me tight. "Say you are mine," he pleaded again.

"Dimitri," I whispered, "I am mine. But you may feed from me."

He groaned, leaning me against the wall. My arms wrapped around his neck. I kissed him deeply, feeling his energy seeping into me. "Take me now," I said.

He entered me slowly, his energy pulsing around us, glowing brighter the deeper he went. He moved slowly, his hands on my face, my body, roaming all over me.

"Harder," I begged, the slowness of it too much for me, burning me with its tease.

His pace quickened, and I held on to him, my mind tumbling, releasing, gaining power. I felt his fangs against my neck and the hint of them, the promise of his bite, sent waves of pleasure through me. "Yes," I whispered—all of it felt so *right*. With my eyes closed against the darkness, I could still see his light and mine twined together, my center pulling from him, taking what I needed.

His fangs sank into me in time with one of his thrusts. The pleasure was so intense I didn't even make a sound. Colors exploded around us as he drank from me, taking from me as I took from him, a circle of energy that seemed to grow stronger with every suck, each thrust, every breath.

My heart banged, pushing blood through me, to him. Dimitri's heart thumped, then it began to beat with mine as his thrusts became more frantic, his lips tightening against me, and I felt his release as if it were my own.

Energy exploded between us, filling the small space, expanding out of the room and then collapsing back into us, jolting his fangs from my neck, almost knocking us to the ground. But Dimitri steadied himself with one hand, keeping the other around me.

His forehead against mine, Dimitri breathed steadily, his heart beating, my blood moving through his veins. "What is happening to me?" he asked.

I cupped his face, letting my thumb cross his lips, feeling my own blood there. "I don't know."

He leaned down and licked at my neck, but there were no wounds to heal. I'd closed them on my own.

We dressed in clean clothing Dimitri found in the apartment. Jeans and a T-shirt for me. A pair of too-large underpants. He could not find a bra to fit me. *Why not take on a hive of vampires with my tits out?*

I didn't see Dimitri's outfit until we were back out on the street in the last of the moonlight—a gray T-shirt that hugged his shoulders and a pair of worn jeans. I stared at him. His hair slicked back, skin like polished porcelain, ice blue chips of color buried in his gray eyes. *He looks even better casual than in a suit.*

I could hear his heartbeat slowing…fading. How long until it stopped again?

"Come." He looked east toward the horizon. "We must go." He picked me up, blurring through the streets, passing too quickly for any danger that would seek to harm us. I closed my eyes against the wind and leaned my face into his solid chest, feeling safe and cherished. *Only my father and Megan ever made me feel so at home.*

He stopped in front of a large plantation house in need of a paint job. Three stories tall, the marble entrance featured large corniced columns. The whole thing was lit up like there was a party inside, but it was quiet. Dimitri put me down. As our feet crunched over the gravel, I stopped for a second. "What?" Dimitri asked.

"Do they want to kill me?" I asked.

He shook his head. "They want to turn you. To save you. They do not know you are different."

"Are you going to tell them?" He shook his head. "Thank you."

Dimitri reached out and took my hand. "I like touching you too much." He gave me a rueful smile.

"Even though I'll never be yours."

"I have not given up on that yet." His smile faded. *The vampire is determined. But so am I.* "You make me...I cannot explain it, Darling. You make me feel." He looked down at our hands. "That is something I have not done in a long time." Dimitri brought his eyes to meet mine again. "I have existed for eight centuries, but before you, I don't think I ever lived." His words stole my breath away. He stepped closer, our bodies flush. "I won't let anyone hurt you. Ever." *That sounds like a vow.*

"You are mine." I claimed him somehow, not clear what it meant, but knowing that it was true.

His lips twitched into a smile, and he cupped my cheek, leaning in to kiss me, gently at first, but it deepened so that I wrapped one of my legs around his waist, and he gripped me as if someone was trying to tear me away. His energy poured into me. I broke away, panting. "You need your strength." He nodded, our foreheads touching.

We walked up the marble steps, and Dimitri opened the door. The living room was empty, but Megan appeared quickly. "You're okay? Were you bitten?"

Her beauty struck me again: the vibrance of her red hair, her glowing skin, the fear I could see in her eyes making her even more gorgeous— desperate but definitely alive.

"I'm fine," I said. "But, Megan—" I grabbed her hands, so cold and smooth, like the marble I was standing on. "I need to talk to you. There is so much I've learned."

Megan bit her lip and looked over her shoulder. "There's no time."

Pearl, her long blonde hair tied up into a high ponytail, exposing her long, elegant neck, floated into the room. The navy blue shirt she wore scooped across her shoulders, exposing defined collarbones. Her light blue eyes, those cold orbs, focused on Megan. "Come," she said, waving to us. "We must begin your transformation, Darling."

"I don't want to change," I said. *For the first time in my life.*

Pearl laughed shifting her gaze to me. "Oh good. So you want to donate? Or did you want to die?" She smiled.

I shook my head. "I want to stay alive, for as long as I can, as a human. Just let me go. Let Megan come with me."

Pearl's face darkened. "Who are *you* to give me orders?" Her voice was quiet and powerful, her influence sliding across the room to me. I let it settle over me, keeping the center of me under my own control.

Pearl blurred across the room, her fingers digging into my biceps as she dragged me across the space. My feet stumbled, and I fell over the old carpet; the only thing keeping me upright was Pearl. She pushed me through a door and dropped me onto the floor in front of Megan's father, Brad.

He leaned against a large wooden desk, an almost bored expression on his handsome face. The walls of the room were lined with bookshelves filled with leather-bound volumes. Behind the desk was a large window, the heavy drapes closed against the near dawn.

To my left was a table. From my vantage point on the floor, I couldn't see what was on the surface, but three vampires stood around it—two women and one very tall man. They all had that same pale skin, accented by the sweetest pink lips and cheeks. Their blue eyes were just as cold and blue as every other vampire in the room...except Dimitri's, which now flashed with a silver gray that I put there.

Slowly, I climbed to my feet.

Megan's father stared, his influence bearing down on me so that I felt him under my skin. "You don't want the gift we have offered?"

"I want to stay human."

"Then you'll go to the camps. We have no use for a human here." He waved a hand in a *take her away* gesture.

"Just let me go," I said, looking at the floor trying to seem small and harmless.

"Please, Dad," Megan said. "Let us both go."

His gaze left me, and I peeked up from beneath my eyelashes. He stared at the door where Megan stood, her hands pressed together like a prayer. "Please," she said again. "I'll take care of her."

He curled his lip, disgust clear in his features. "You can't survive off one human. Especially not one of your own blood."

"I'll find others," she said.

Pearl spoke up then. "I forbid it. I just got my daughter back. I'm not going to let you go again."

Megan turned to look at her. "Got me back?" She laughed, a hollow, joyless sound. "You abandoned me long before you were turned."

"You would have died if we hadn't come for you," Pearl said.

"Maybe I'd be better off," Megan spat at her mother.

"How dare you," Brad roared, his anger raising him off the ground—he floated on a swirling black cloud of power shot through with sparks of gold. His face contorted with rage.

One of the vampires who'd been standing around the table, a small woman with delicate features and long chestnut hair, spoke softly. "Brad, calm down."

Megan's father's head whipped to her. "Angelia, this is none of your concern."

"And yet here I am hearing all of it." Angelia flapped a hand at me. "Just kill the human and let's get on with it." She turned back to the table, and the tall vampire, a man with blond shoulder-length hair, looked at me, his fangs distending. Megan blurred between us.

"No!" she yelled. "She is of my blood."

Angelia smiled at Megan. "I don't care."

One of the shelves of books seemed to explode, the paper raining down around like confetti. The white shreds appeared to move in slow motion compared to the whirl of bodies that whipped through the space. The desk cracked in half under a weight I could not see.

Megan's body slammed into the wall next to Dimitri, and she fell to the ground, motionless. Brad stood over her limp form. He straightened his shirt and then turned back to me.

"I will drain you myself." He started toward me, his walk slow and predatory.

I backed away, fear clawing at me.

I tried to muster up my power, the ability to stop things in motion, to freeze him. *No, no, no!* I screamed in my head. But he continued his approach. My eyes unfocused, and I looked at the energy in the room, at the influences, the overlapping shapes. Those lines of light that pulled at Dimitri, that seemed to control him, led straight to Brad's heart. His still, dead heart.

I put my hand out, palm facing that organ, and I let the center of me move up, let that little red ball I'd been hiding in my gut flow through my palm and aim at that long-still heart. *Beat.* I told it. *Beat for me.*

Brad reached me, and I placed my hand against his chest. He grinned down at my hand. *So small and weak.*

The vampire's pectoral muscle was hard, his chest cavity still. I closed my eyes and felt the electric connection, the heat building between my palm and his skin through the thin material of the dress shirt.

I opened my eyes and met his gaze—Brad's eyes flashed brown. I reached my lips up to his and he stayed still, shocked and confused as I gently breathed him in.

Closing my eyes, I saw his sphere of control, the way it covered every vampire in the room. *Beat*, I told his heart, pushing that red ball of my own through his skin, through the hard muscle. His heart contracted, and his sphere of influence blinked out, then on again.

"What is she doing?" Angelia asked in a low whisper.

I reached out with my mind, running it along the connection between Brad and Dimitri. It wasn't all smooth—there were joints, spots of intensity that held it together. I stopped on one and tugged. Dimitri gasped. *Break.*

And it did—the line cracked at that point and drifted apart, each side disappearing into ash before it touched the floor.

Brad shuddered, his arms coming up and taking hold of mine, trying to break our kiss. His heart beat again, blinking out the light of his influence.

But while his will wanted me gone, his body, his heart, every organ in his body, wanted me close.

I snapped the next cord leading to Dimitri, and he cried out again.

"Stop her!" Angelia yelled. With my eyes closed, I could see them all —not their bodies but their energy, their abilities—and there wasn't a single one of them that could stop me.

Dimitri, with only one cord left, warned them, "Don't touch her."

"Dimitri!" Pearl's voice went high with panic, her energy vibrating with fear. "Do something!"

I snapped that last cord, using a thump of Brad's heart to do it.

"I am free," Dimitri said, his voice awed. "She has freed me."

"Freed you?" Pearl asked. "What are you talking about?"

I broke the kiss with Brad, and he stumbled away from me and then came back at me, lust clear in his eyes as they flashed brown, human, alive again for the first time in decades.

CHAPTER TWENTY-FIVE

BRAD GRABBED MY ARMS, hauling me up so that we were eye to eye, my feet dangling in the air. Anger and confusion rolled off of him.

His lip snarled, and he threw me. I smashed into a bookshelf. The wood shattered and splinters sliced into me. I slumped on the ground, books raining down on me.

My ears rang and vision swirled. Across the room, Megan still slumped against the opposite wall. Here we were again, I thought, sharing another horrible experience.

Megan lay still, but the three vampires who'd watched the family drama unfold were now in action. Angelia stood in front of Brad, her hand on his neck, feeling for a pulse I knew was no longer there. His eyes were ice blue and burning into me.

The tall male vampire who'd wanted to drain me was gone, the window open, curtains stirring in the breeze. *Smart guy.* The other female vampire, small and elegant with dark hair cut in a pixie style, stood next to Pearl. Both women watched me.

Dimitri blurred to my side and growled at the rest of the room, like a dog protecting his bone. I tried to push myself up, but dizziness overtook me, and I waited, closing my eyes, trying to regain my strength, knowing there was only one way to really recover.

Dimitri scooped me up into his arms, and his influence settled over me, taking away the pain from my bruises and cuts. "I will take her," he said. "I will keep her safe."

"You will do no such thing." Brad stepped forward, his eyes cold again, his heart still but his dick throbbing for me. I could *feel* the war inside of him. One part wanted me desperately, and the other part knew I was dangerous. *Maybe that's why he wants me so much. Maybe we all seek danger.* "We need to figure out what she is." He pointed at me. "That is no normal girl."

"She is mine," Dimitri said.

Brad smiled. "She is Megan's. You cannot claim her."

"Who will stop me?"

I wanted to be a part of the conversation. Explain that I belonged to myself, but there was a gash on the back of my head seeping blood. I needed to heal before I lost consciousness. But I wasn't leaving this place without Megan. She was the reason I came back. She was my best friend, and I wasn't about to give her up a second time.

"I want Megan," I said, my voice weak, spots clouding my vision. "She has to come with us, Dimitri."

He didn't look down at me, just kept staring straight ahead at Brad. The other vampires fanned out behind their leader, his influence lining them up, settling into a triangle behind him, blocking our escape.

I looked back up at Dimitri, black edging into the corners of my vision. "Kiss me," I whispered.

He didn't respond—couldn't take his eyes off the vamps in front of us. *He will have to fight them all.* "Megan," I whispered, looking over at her, willing her to wake up. She stayed still, eyes closed, face smooth and emotionless…like a doll.

Brad glanced back at her and then made eye contact with me. "I control her, Darling. I don't know what you are, but it is impossible for you to take my daughter from me."

I held his gaze and smiled. "Kiss me." Brad took a step forward. Pearl grabbed his arm. "Keep coming." My eyes held his. *I'm going to black out soon. I need a kiss.* I needed more than one.

"Don't look at her." Pearl grabbed her husband's chin and turned it toward her, breaking our connection. "No one meet her gaze," Pearl warned.

I closed my eyes, the blood loss becoming too much. I'd hit my head too hard. I was in many respects still a weak human. *Megan,* I begged in my mind. *Wake up, Megan. Wake up!* I pushed my thoughts out of my body with what I had left, blowing them across the room, settling them over her. *Wake up.*

She stirred, her energy reacting to mine. Behind my closed lids I saw her brain light up, coming awake, wrestling from under her father's influence. The cords connecting them were far too strong for me to break, as weak as I was, but she fluttered her eyes. And then they opened with mine.

I stared across the room at her, and she smiled at me, her moss green eye glowing with her love for me. Megan climbed to her feet like a puppet whose strings were being pulled taut. "Stay where you are, Megan," Brad said. "You're not going anywhere. Neither are you, Dimitri."

All the vampires in the room turned to the open window. "My God," Dimitri whispered.

They were transfixed, staring out the large window behind the now-broken desk. All I could see was darkness.

Dimitri and I were blown back, my body flying through the air. I was aloft so long I had time to think about how much it was going to hurt when I landed. *A lot.*

But then Dimitri caught me again. I hung over his shoulder, blood dripping off my fingers as we moved at an insane speed—everything around me a blur. Another blow, and I fell onto the marble steps, my forearm cracking as it broke under my body's weight. The pain sliced through me and I cried out.

Two bodies, maybe more, fought in the yard—moving too fast for me to see. An arm came around my neck and pulled me up, cutting off my air supply, making me forget about the scorching pain in my arm.

"What are you?" Pearl whispered harshly into my ear.

"Put her down," a voice boomed—it not only filled the yard but also echoed inside my head. The weight against my throat slacked and my toes touched the ground again.

Pearl pushed me away, and I fell to my knees, my good arm still clasping my broken one. I looked back at Pearl. Her gaze was riveted to the woods. Next to her, the other two female vampires stared in the same direction, Megan pinned between them, her gaze also focused on the trees.

In the yard, Dimitri held Brad around the neck—they looked as if they'd been frozen in time and space.

The brush rustled, and I strained my eyes trying to see into the darkness. From between two of the old oak trees, a man appeared. He wore mud-encrusted clothing, his hair stiff with the same hardened dirt. As he stepped out of the deep shadows, I stopped breathing. "Emmanuel," I whispered.

All the vampires dropped to their knees and bowed their heads. Dimitri and Brad next to each other, no longer fighting, both supplicating to my bassist. *What in the what?*

He walked slowly up to me. "I told you to wait for me," he said. "You are hurt," Emmanuel frowned, laying his hand onto my broken arm. I flinched at his touch.

He dipped his head and brushed his lips against mine. I reached for him, hungry for the connection. He smiled, just out of my reach, and then slowly pressed his lips to mine, his tongue darting out. I moaned against him as I felt the bones moving inside my body, reconnecting with a sickening crunch. I whimpered more because of how strange it felt than anything else.

He pulled back, and I stumbled forward, off balance from the kiss. He caught me, tucking me into his side, and I looked up at him. There were no wounds at his neck.

Emmanuel looked fine, great in fact—even with the dirt covering his body and the leaves sticking out of his hair. He squeezed me and then looked down at Pearl. "You were lucky I did not find her more injured." His gaze traveled over the rest of the vampires.

Dimitri stood, his head still bowed. "Will you allow me to serve you?" he asked. *Serve Emmanuel? What is going on?*

Emmanuel laced his fingers through mine and energy passed between us, growing stronger with each exchange. *How is this happening?*

He brought me to where Dimitri stood.

"Did you feed from her?" Emmanuel asked.

I felt my face flush at the memories. "Yes," Dimitri answered, keeping his gaze on the ground. A gash on his shoulder dyed his T-shirt red. My fingers itched to comfort him.

"He saved me," I said. "I'd be dead if it weren't for Dimitri."

Emmanuel looked down at me. "You may serve her," he said to Dimitri but still looking at me. "Can you do that?"

"If it pleases you, my Lord."

"Are you a vampire?" I whispered to Emmanuel. He laughed low in his throat.

Dimitri's eyes flicked to my face. "He is the son of our Lord. He died for our sins."

"What?" A laugh bubbled out of me, remembering Tyronios's words. *Wait.* Emmanuel was the being he spoke of, the creature who might be spreading zombism for his own benefit? *The man they hunted.*

Tyronios also thought that my ancestor started the zombie plague to begin with, so how could I trust him? But my father did...Emmanuel brushed a kiss across my forehead. Warmth and goodness exuded from him. *Can I trust my instincts? What else do I have?*

"If I had known—" Brad started to say.

"Shut up," Emmanuel snapped. "You tried to kill her, despite being of the same blood." He shook his head. "Should I take your life?"

Brad didn't answer, just bowed his head further, exposing the back of his neck—as if offering it.

Emmanuel slid his hand over my hip and rested it on the hilt of my knife. "What do you say, Darling? Should I let him live or send him on to the final death?" *Just your run of the mill first date question.* I suppressed an insane laugh.

"Let him live," I said. "But make him release Megan." *Maybe on our next date we'll have a human sacrifice.*

Emmanuel smiled at me. "Magic has chosen well for me." *What did he just say?* Emmanuel returned his attention to Brad. "Release your daughter."

"Yes, of course," Brad kept his gaze toward the ground. "Megan," he said, his voice strong, "I release you of all obligation and ties. You are your own."

I saw the lines between them snap and drift toward the ground, disappearing before they touched the earth. Megan let out a sharp breath of surprise.

Emmanuel turned to Dimitri. "I give you in service to Darling Price." Dimitri dropped to his knees at my side. "Do you accept him?" he asked.

I looked around at the vampires with their heads bowed. "What does it mean?" I whispered.

"They can hear you," Emmanuel whispered back, leaning close to me. He smelled like fresh-turned soil.

I cleared my throat, raising my voice. "Well, then, what does it mean?" I tilted my head toward Dimitri, "what does 'in service' mean?"

"He will do anything to keep you safe."

"He already does that."

"Why?"

I didn't answer. Emmanuel's face darkened, and he turned to Dimitri. "Why do you protect her?"

"I love her," he answered, his voice calm and ringing with truth. Emmanuel's hand tightened on my hip, jealousy sparking in his eyes. Dimitri looked toward the road. "Lord," he said.

"Yes, I hear them," Emmanuel said. "It is the warlocks. We must go, Darling." He took my hand and began to lead me to the woods. *I guess Tyronios's found his man.*

"Hold on," I said, trying to stop, but Emmanuel held me fast. "Hey!" I stumbled after him. Dimitri followed, and Megan ran down the steps to join us. At the forest's edge, Emmanuel turned back to Brad, who remained on his knees. "Hold them off," Emmanuel said. "If they reach us, I will make you pay."

I tried to pull away again. "What are you doing?" I asked. "Just hold on a second. I need to understand what is going on here."

"Trust me?" Emmanuel looked down into my eyes, his hair falling over his face so I had that sensation again, that it was just the two of us in this whole world. "Trust me that I will never hurt you," he said. "That I will always cherish you. That I have come to this world for you, and I'm not leaving without you."

I stared up at him, speechless. *This seems more like ninth date kind of stuff.*

Brad yelled commands. I looked back—cars speed into the driveway, rocking on their shocks as they stopped. Men in robes, wands in their hands, piled out of the cars, sparkles of light and clouds of yellow smoke spilling out with them.

Emmanuel pulled me into the woods. Dimitri and Megan followed. They would keep me safe. I stumbled over a root, and Emmanuel picked me up as he hurried down the hill toward a stream.

176

I heard a scream behind us and looked over Emmanuel's shoulder. Bursts of light flashed through the trees. He waded into the water with me still in his arms, Dimitri and Megan close.

A robed figure ran between the trees. He raised a wand at us. *A freaking wand!* Light shot out of it, headed straight for us.

My vision swirled, changing the forest around us into just a whirl of colors. I felt a sucking sensation, my body stretching and pulling. Time slowed down, particles floated across my vision: tree bark, leaves, the filtered light of dawn, all reflected off of diamonds suspended in space.

Then nothing. No beginning, no ending. No me.

I reformed, my body coming back together, and we stood in the stream again but the robed figure was gone, the house was gone, the road gone.

I looked around. Megan and Dimitri flanked us. Emmanuel smiled, his arms warm around me. "Welcome to my world. Welcome home," he said.

Turn the page for a sneak peek of *Dark Secret*, The Kiss Chronicles Book 2.

SNEAK PEEK

DARK SECRET, THE KISS CHRONICLES BOOK 2

Birds sang, welcoming the rising sun. Emmanuel smiled, his arms warm around me. "Welcome to my world. Welcome home."

He stepped up onto the bank and set me down, my feet sinking into soft, wet earth. "Where are we?" Dimitri asked, still standing in the swiftly moving stream, looking up to where the house was only moments ago. *A mere flash ago.* But now, it was just trees—ancient, snarled trees, ferns at their feet. A forest untouched by development. *Impossible.*

Emmanuel did not answer, his hand trailing along my waist for a moment before he returned to the water, walking deeper into it as he pulled off his dirt-encrusted shirt.

Faint rays of the rising sun lit his exposed skin, playing over the defined muscles in his back and tangling in his curls that were stiff with dried mud. "We are...in a different dimension, aren't we?" I asked.

"What?" Megan's voice was quiet.

Emmanuel twisted, his broad shoulders angling toward me. My eyes caught on the V shape of muscles below his tight abdominals. *Dear Lord.* That's what they called him...the vampires all called him Lord.

Emmanuel gave me a devastating smile, his eyes promising a reward for my observational powers. Tingles of anticipation raced over my skin.

Bending down, Emmanuel dunked his shirt beneath the swiftly moving water. Megan joined me on the bank, her brilliant red hair catching the light. My heart rate picked up. "Dimitri and Megan can't be in the sunlight."

It filtered through the trees, imbuing this new world with a soft golden flush, but soon it would pierce through the foliage—rays of light that were deadly to Dimitri and Megan.

Emmanuel moved to a deeper part of the stream and dropped to his knees, then submerged himself into the frigid water. Dirt flowed off of him, a brown cloud carried away by the current.

Dimitri joined Megan and me at the water's edge, his shoes sinking into the moist dirt. The T-shirt he wore was ripped and blood stained, yet he still moved like a dancer, all controlled elegance. His pale blue eyes avoided mine, looking into the distance instead. "There is a cave," he said. "About a mile that way." He nodded his chin toward the rising sun. "At least there was in our world. We should go now, Megan."

I wanted to cup his cheek and turn him toward me. So much had changed in such a short period of time. We were lovers just hours ago. And now, Emmanuel had made him my…what? Protector, servant? *Either way, he wasn't looking at me.*

"I'm not leaving Darling," Megan said, crossing her arms over her stomach and setting her jaw, her mismatched eyes hard.

"She will be safe," Dimitri assured her. "Emmanuel is here."

Emmanuel sat up then, water dripping off him as he rose, his skin prickling from the cold water and fresh air. He shook his head and droplets sprayed, catching the early morning light, looking like jewels.

He approached us and handed Dimitri his shirt, without looking at the vampire. "Wring this out for me." *Would saying please kill the man… Lord…whatever the hell he was.*

Dimitri took the shirt and twisted it, his forearm muscles coming into relief as water splattered onto the muddy shore. "Thank you," Emmanuel said, a playful smile twisting his lips. *Did he read my mind?* "Go to the cave," he waved at Megan. "We will meet you there at sunset." When she made no move to leave, Emmanuel focused his attention on her. She dropped her gaze. "Do not fear," he said, his voice low. "Darling is in good hands."

Megan chewed on her lip and gave a small nod. "Just…" She sighed, reaching out and taking my hand. "I'll see you soon. You'll be okay, right?" I nodded, and she squeezed my fingers. *She was so cold, so inhuman.*

I turned to Dimitri and caught his eye, reaching out with my influence. *He burned with the urge to touch me.* I reached for him, and he moved blindingly fast, wrapping me in his arms, one hand buried in my hair, the other spanning my low back. I melted against the hard lines and smooth planes of his chest. His lips brushed my forehead. While not chaste, the embrace bore none of the heat roiling inside of him.

Emmanuel controlled the ancient vampire, keeping him at bay, stopping him from feeding me.

Dimitri released me, and the two vampires blurred out of sight. Emmanuel stepped closer, his chest still bare, his jeans wet and clinging to him. He took my hand, lacing our fingers, and warmth spread over me. I shivered at the sudden heat. "What are we?" I asked. "What are you to me?"

"I hope to be your everything," he answered.

"I don't understand." I looked down at his hand. *We almost screwed on a concession table at a club before our last performance.* We'd only played together for a few months. And now suddenly we were destined to be together forever? "How long have you known what I am?"

"I wasn't sure, not until that day."

"Which day?"

"The one you were just thinking about." I heard a smile in his voice. "The last time we played together." The way he said *played* didn't make it sound like he was talking about music.

"Can you read my mind?" I met his eyes—the warm brown of tree bark glinting with sparkles of amethyst. Water dripped from his hair, the rivulets sliding down his neck and over his collarbones to his chest. *And what an incredible chest it was...*

He chuckled—a warm, masculine sound. "I can't stop thinking about it. I have not stopped thinking about you. You are meant for me. I am sure of it."

I shook my head, trying to clear the haze of lust fogging my thoughts. "There are so many people who think they know what I am—know some kind of destiny for me."

He squeezed my hand. "Yes, but don't you feel it?" Energy pulsed from him and ran over my skin. I shivered, my eyes fluttering closed. *Oh, I felt it.* But on the heels of that wave of desire fear followed—the avalanche behind the gunshot. *Don't get crushed.*

Emmanuel placed his big hand on my hip, pulling me just a tiny bit closer. His head bent down. "Don't be scared, Darling," he whispered, so close that his words felt like a caress. My eyes opened and met his. "I will never hurt you," he promised, his gaze intense. "I will never let anyone hurt you." His fingers flexed possessively on my hip.

His words were as effective as a bullet, striking me in the chest, hitting me square in all the feels. *I've always wanted protection.* I'd lived most my life hiding…but…*here comes the suffocating avalanche.* "Will you try to decide my future for me?" I asked, my voice small. I hated how weak I sounded. *How much I wanted the protection he promised.*

A soft, knowing smile played over Emmanuel's lips, and he shook his head. "Your destiny is your own. I have no power to control it. And neither do you."

I bit my lip. *Was that true?* Energy thrummed between us. *I wanted so much.* Control over my own life, to be safe, Emmanuel to touch me, to make sense of all that happened…but that was impossible. There was no making sense of this world. *It wasn't even my world.* "What did you mean by calling this place home?" I asked, grasping at straws.

He didn't answer me. Our gaze locked. The scent of honey rose up between us. It would only take a small movement for our lips to meet, but neither of us made it.

There was something truly delicious about this moment all on its own —not touching, except where his warm palm rested against my hip. It was like the seconds before a performance—a tantalizing anticipation. *The moment before the snow slips down the side of the mountain.* Once we tip over the edge, there will be no going back.

The energy strained to be released, building up inside of us so that it seemed to fill the forest. Our influences combined, floating into and through one another, mixing so that I could barely tell where one began and the other ended.

I stared into his eyes, sinking into him. Emmanuel had access to every part of me, and I to him. There was no hiding from one another. This would not be a race to satisfaction like I felt with Dimitri, not a ravaging hunger, but a slow and luxurious meal we would share. Music filled my ears, a tune I didn't know but recognized. "What is that sound?" I whispered.

Emmanuel's free hand circled my other hip. He slowly, achingly, folded the space between us into nothingness. His wet jeans pressed against my dry ones, and I resented all the clothing I'd ever worn.

He lowered his lips, my eyes slipped closed. His mouth against mine was warm and soft, hungry but controlled. I let my hands run up his arms, feeling every muscle as I passed over it, reveling in his form as my fingers wound up and into his hair.

Our kiss deepened.

Colors splashed behind my eyes, and power rose between us, shaking the trees, making the stream run faster, pulling energy from the air and filling us with it. *Yes, I felt it.*

His hands slipped under my shirt, caressing my bare skin. I shivered from the pleasure of his touch, reveling in the power he shared with me.

"Yes," I whispered. "Yes." I didn't know what I was agreeing to. I'd slipped over the edge, the mountain of snow began its descent—watch out below!

My legs wobbled from all the power coursing through us. I leaned into him, under his control as he kissed me again, his tongue diving into me, driving more energy into me, filling me up so that every cell in my body vibrated.

That song—I recognized it.

It rose as the aches and pains from the wounds I'd sustained healed, as if they'd never been there. He took away any pain I'd *ever* had, any hurt; everything bad floated away like the dirt he'd washed off in the stream—a cloud whisked into nothingness by a strong current.

All the atoms in the universe vibrate in the same frequency, and now I could hear it.

"Sorry to interrupt." A voice broke through our passion. Emmanuel's hands gripped me tighter. "Emmanuel!" A hot and sharp spark snapped between us. breaking our kiss.

Emmanuel growled. "How dare you?"

"Is that how you talk to your wife?"

Wife?

Continue reading *Dark Secret*, The Kiss Chronicles Book 2: emilykimelman.com/ERDSwb.

A NOTE FROM EMILY

Thanks so much for reading *Lost Secret*! I'm grateful you took a chance on the first book in this new series and liked it enough to make it all the way to my note.

I'd appreciate it if you would leave a review with your thoughts. It's super helpful to other readers who wonder if this book is for them. We wouldn't want someone who thinks zombies are gross and sex should be hidden to read this—they'd hate it! But someone who loves fast paced urban fantasy with strong romance themes—this is their *thing*.

Turn the page to learn more about my mystery and thriller books I release under my own name.

Thank you for joining me on this new adventure!

Thank you,
Emily

ABOUT THE AUTHOR

Emily Reed is the pen name of Emily Kimelman. That's me! I write romances full of adventure as Emily Reed and mystery-thrillers with grit as Emily Kimelman.

I'm married to a wonderful man and have two awesome kids. My husband and I both have serious cases of wanderlust and while children have slowed our roll, we still manage to hit the open road regularly. I get my best story ideas while traveling but do my best writing while alone—there is dancing involved that no one wants to see, and occasionally I'll even do the worm in-between writing sprints. ;-)

Want to try one of my mystery thrillers? Get a free copy of *Unleashed*, the first book in my Sydney Rye series for free when you join my email list: emilykimelman.com/newsletter.

Want to stay in touch about my romances and urban fantasies and always know when I have a new Emily Reed release: emilykimelman.com/ERNews.

EMILY'S BOOKSHELF

Visit www.emilyreedbooks.com for a complete list.

EMILY REED

ROMANCES

The Kiss Chronicles

Lost Secret

Dark Secret

Stolen Secret

Buried Secret

(Coming 2021)

EMILY KIMELMAN

MYSTERIES & THRILLERS

Sydney Rye Mysteries

Unleashed

Death in the Dark

Insatiable

Strings of Glass

The Devil's Breath

Inviting Fire

Shadow Harvest

The Girl with the Gun

In Sheep's Clothing

Flock of Wolves

Betray the Lie

Savage Grace

Blind Vigilance

Fatal Breach

(Coming 2021)

Starstruck Thrillers

A Spy is Born